The Gift of Something Grand

Jamett & Joseph Series, Book Three

Renee Vincent

writing as
Gracie Lee Rose

THE GIFT OF SOMETHING GRAND
Copyright © 2014, Renee Vincent writing as Gracie Lee Rose
Digital ISBN: 9780985583149
Trade Paperback ISBN: 9780985583156

Cover Art Design: Renee Vincent
Editors: Karen Block

For God,
whose blessings upon me number like the stars.

For my wonderful editor, Karen
While I brought the details of the story to the table, you put it all in a much broader context, encouraging me to strive for a deeper heroine's point of view. Between the two of us, a great story was born. I cannot thank you enough for your tireless attention to detail and supportive guidance in the past few months. Thank you for being there for me.

Acknowledgements

I'd like to take this opportunity to thank my adoring fans—particularly Lysette Lam and Patty Lacey, who helped me name one of my characters in this series. They suggested the name Miranda (Randi) for my hero's oldest sister and, after careful consideration of more than fifty names offered by my newsletter followers, I totally fell in love with their choice. Thank you both for your clever insight and creativity.

I'd also like to give thanks to my fellow Ink Heart authors for all their support, promotional posts, and of course their graciousness. Thank you especially to *New York Times* and *USA Today* bestselling authors Suzanne Rock and Opal Carew. Your friendship and limitless generosity mean so much to me, and I cannot thank you enough for taking me under your wing. I will never forget what you've done for me.

THE GIFT OF SOMETHING GRAND

When those three little words aren't enough.

Jamie Sutherland finds herself falling in love with her irresistible next-door neighbor, Joseph Scarbrough. No surprise there. But when she wakes up in his bed, she's stunned that even in her sleep, she can't resist him.

As their relationship heats up, Joseph gives Jamie a key to his apartment and he finally gives Caroline, his relentless ex-girlfriend, the boot. Jamie's excited to think he just might be *the one*.

But how do you tell the man of your dreams you love him when he insists that he can't fall in love?

Chapter One

"Why am I in your bed? Think again, Sutherland. You're in mine."

Joseph Scarbrough's words hit me like a ton of bricks. My eyes scanned the room. I fell asleep in a mint green room last night and woke up this morning in a blue one. I was, indeed, in his bed.

But how'd I get in here? Did he really beckon for me in the middle of the night and I succumbed? I wouldn't do that. *Would I?*

I watched him run his fingers through his bedhead crop of hair. His bare chest looked richly appealing against the crisp white sheets. I now cursed my overactive imagination because now was not the time to be weak.

"Seriously, Joseph. Why am I in this room?"

"Hell, if I know." He propped himself up on one elbow. "It was about four in the morning when you came in, and I was too tired to care."

Sheer panic tightened its vise around my heart. "I sleep walked?" What if I had also talked in my sleep? What if I said things to him? Things I'd never divulge this soon in a relationship. Scratch that. I didn't want to know. I just needed to get away.

I jumped from the bed and took the covers with me. "I can't believe I did this. I'm so sorry." Brisk air met my bare legs, and I fumbled to cover them with the blankets. I knew I should've slept in my own pants and not just the oversized T-shirt Joseph had given me. "Why didn't you kick me out?"

"Yeah, 'cause that's what we men do. We wine and dine women in hope you'll climb into bed with us—just so we can kick you out."

I heard his quiet laughter as I hustled toward the door right before he leapt from the bed and caught me at the threshold. In his boxer briefs. At least I didn't have to wonder anymore.

"Hey, you don't have to be sorry. Trust me, I didn't mind."

I squeezed my eyes shut. My face flamed with embarrassment. I was not one of those girls who jumped into bed with a guy. To me, an intimate relationship was something further down the line, when both parties were committed and ready. Sure, I was committed and ready, but I was pretty darn sure he wasn't. "That's not the point, Joseph. I'm not like this. I don't hop into bed with men— *especially* this soon and—"

"Hey," he interrupted, brushing my tangled hair from my face. "Nothing happened. I promise. I was a perfect gentleman."

I gritted my teeth and forced a smile. Maybe he was, but what was I? I had no recollection of my actions and I feared I may have come on too strong. "I'm not worried about what you did or didn't do. I know you wouldn't take advantage of me but what did I—"

"Jamie, breathe." He gave me a little shake and looked deep into my eyes. I relaxed at the sight of that calm Montana blue sky staring back at me and sighed. His lovely blue eyes could ground me every time.

"That's better. Now listen. I was taught never to wake a sleep walker. God only knows why we're taught that, but, frankly, I wouldn't have wakened you up anyway. It was obvious you had no idea what you were doing. You were cute."

"Cute?"

"Yes, cute. Especially when you snuggled your little butt against me."

I sighed even heavier this time. "Great. Just great." I tried to walk away, dragging the blankets and my shredded dignity with me, but he stopped me again.

"Sutherland, wait. I know you're embarrassed about this, but you don't have to be. Nothing happened."

"I know, but it's your sister's house."

"And my sister's house gets drafty. You were cold. Besides, she probably has no idea this even happened in the first place. You're freaking out for nothing."

"I guess."

Joseph must have heard the skepticism in my voice. He pulled me into his arms, blankets and all, and hugged me. "It could've happen to anyone. In fact, I can think of no better person I'd want sleep walking into my bed. In the words of Keith Urban, you look *good* in my shirt."

I felt his hand on the bare skin of my thigh where the blankets had failed to cover me. I pushed him away and hobbled into the bedroom across the hall. I tried to keep myself shielded with the swath of blankets wrapped around me, but was failing miserably.

He blew out a perfect construction worker's whistle. "Nice legs, Sutherland."

I slammed the door and collapsed against it, beaming with delight behind the safety of the wood. My brain was in a complete whirlwind, and I couldn't have been happier. The sexiest eligible bachelor I'd ever known had just favored me with a sexist whistle and I loved it.

Chapter Two

A light knock sounded on the door behind my head. "You want to take a shower?"

My breath caught. Instant pictures of Joseph and me, all wet and soapy, filled my brain. Surely he didn't mean *with* him...

"Separate, of course," he added after I hadn't responded.

I breathed a little easier. "That would be nice."

"Ladies first," he offered.

"No, you go ahead. I've got to....um...." I needed time to myself. To get a grip. A serious grip. "I need to call work and see if everything's okay. Make sure they don't need me to come in."

"If you say so." I know that was disappointment I heard in his voice. "I'll set out a towel and washcloth for you when I'm finished."

"Thanks." I didn't really need to call work. Donna, my college weekend crew leader, had my number and never hesitated to call if things went haywire. I did, however, want to call my grandmother. She'd given me such good advice about taking that risk with Joseph that I thought it only fair to let her know how the date went.

I heaved my blanket-cocooned self from the door, shuffled to the edge of the bed and plopped down. I reached for my purse and dug out my cell. As I swiped the screen on my iPhone, I heard the water from the shower turn on and figured I had about ten minutes.

I continued to scroll for my grandma's thumbnail and tapped it. I gave her plenty of time to get to the phone. She wasn't as quick as she used to be. After six rings, her cheery voice sounded in my ear.

"Hey, Grandma. It's me."

"Well, hello, Jamie. How are you this morning?"

I fiddled with a loose string on the hem of the blanket draped over my lap. "I took that leap of faith last night."

"You did?" She sounded like she pretended to be shocked, all the while knowing darn good and well that I would. "How did it go?"

I flopped to my back and grinned like a baboon. I had no intention of telling her about how I sleep walked into Joseph's bedroom. Given how important it was to her for a young lady to preserve her reputation, it was probably best to leave that part out. "Oh, Grandma, he pulled out all the stops." I used an expression I knew she'd be familiar with. I seemed to do that often with her as she enjoyed hearing her vintage vernacular still in use.

"This is that Joseph fellow, right?"

"Yeah, that's the one." I imagined her taking a seat on the antique, upholstered chair next to the entryway table that held her black, rotary phone and stain glass lamp.

"So, what made you decide this all of a sudden? Last I heard, you gave up on men. Protecting your fragile heart and all that. What makes this gentleman caller so special?"

I loved the way she referred to Joseph. Just hearing her talk of gentlemen callers and courting made me wish some things were still the same. Back in her day, men were held to gentlemanly standards. It was part of their upbringing; opening doors, standing when a gal entered the room, and pushing her chair in as she sat at the table. It was all second nature. Nowadays, guys barely even walk a girl to her door. In my opinion, not since before the whole equal rights thing started in the nineteen sixties had men been gentlemen. Grandma wasn't the only one who believed times had changed and not necessarily for the better.

"Well, let's see. He's kind and he's funny." I rolled over onto my stomach and crossed my ankles as I continued to tick off his most endearing traits one by one. "He loves his family. He's a musician. He can fix a lot of things, too—he's the building's superintendent. Oh! And he loves your lasagna recipe."

"All good qualities. But what does he look like? Attraction's important too, you know."

I had to laugh. My grandmother may have been in her eighties, but she wasn't a prude. I tried to remember my days watching old black and white movies with her, so I could come up with a handsome actor who most resembled Joseph. "Name some leading Hollywood men, Grandma."

"James Dean? You youngins still think he hung the moon."

"No, too bad-boy looking."

"Okay, how about Clark Gable?"

"No, not him. Can't get passed the mustache."

"Hm. You're a tough cookie. All right, how about Archibald Leach."

"Who?"

I heard Grandma sigh. "Cary Grant, child. Cary Grant."

"Close…Joseph definitely has his casual confidence, but Grant's eyes are too dark. Joseph's are blue. Dreamy blue, like a Montana sky."

"Blue, huh? How about Peter O'Toole then?"

"No, too thin in the face." I twirled a strand of hair around my finger and pondered hard. "Hey, what's that movie we watched with Ava Gardner I really liked?"

"Oh, you mean *The Snows of Kilimanjaro*."

"Yeah, that's the one."

I could almost hear my grandmother's thoughts churning. "You say your Joseph looks like Gregory Peck as Harry Street? Well, now there's a striking man. I'm going to have to meet this Joseph and judge for myself."

"Personally, I think you'll agree, Grandma. He's got that suave demeanor, a chiseled face with a little bit of scruff around his lips, and a darling chunk of hair that always seems to fall over his forehead, just like Harry Street on safari."

"Good hair, you say?"

Grandma was a fan of men with thick hair, claiming she married Grandpa for that very reason. "Oh, the best hair," I crooned. "The kind you can run your fingers through endlessly—"

"Ahem."

Startled, I whirled on the bed and saw Joseph leaning against the doorframe, his arms crossed—a classic young Gregory Peck look—if Peck had ever sported snug Wrangler jeans and a white T. I marveled at how it stretched and fit ever so deliciously across his broad shoulders. He looked like an angel trapped in a bad-boy, Harley-biker body. And his devilish smile said he'd heard every word of my conversation.

I felt my skin flush as I heard Grandma still chattering on the other end. I was pretty sure she was going on about Grandpa's thick head of hair in his younger days, before he went off to war and they buzzed it all off regulation style.

"Um, Grandma," I stuttered, inch-worming off the bed. I kicked at the blankets to free my feet. "I gotta let you go. Can I call you back later?"

"Sure. Is everything all right?"

I heard the concern in her voice and didn't want her to worry. "Everything's fine. Something...pressing just came up." I laid my fingers over my lips to signal Joseph to be silent.

"I hope it's nothing serious," I heard my grandmother say as he sauntered up closer to me, tugging me in his arms.

He murmured in my ear, making me shiver. "Am I really that pressing? I thought I was suave and chiseled with great hair."

I covered his mouth with my palm and widened my eyes at him for emphasis. "No, Grandma, nothing serious at all. Promise."

"If you say so, dear. Stop by and see me sometime."

I hated to rush her, but I needed to get off the phone. Joseph was nibbling my ear and I was extremely ticklish. Holding back a giggle, I pushed him away from my sensitive lobe and told my grandmother I'd visit soon.

Ending the call, I tipped my head back to get a good look at Joseph's face.

His gorgeous, blue eyes twinkled amid a bright toothy grin. His hunky boy-next-door smile was definitely his best asset. That and his muscled chest and arms. And derriere, if we were breaking him down into pieces.

Joseph must have realized I was ogling. "What?"

"Nothing," I lied, delighting in the clean manly smell of the body wash he used. "Just admiring you."

"Oh, yeah?" He gave his head a good shake, causing his too-sexy-for-his-own-good hair to fall over his eye. "Want to admire my darling chunk of hair that you could run your hands through endlessly," he mocked in his best swooning Jamie Sutherland voice.

"Shut up."

Without warning, he dipped his head and I dodged him. "What are you doing?"

"I was going to kiss you."

"No, you're not. I haven't brushed my teeth, Joseph."

"I don't care."

"I do. There's some things a woman doesn't like to reveal."

"Like she has dragon breath in the morning?" He laughed. "It's quite common, Jamie. Everyone has it. Even me."

"I know, but—"

"Here," he said, pulling a brand new toothbrush out of his back pocket. "Brush up, if it'll make you feel better."

I looked at the dental instrument in his hand, still sealed in its package. I accepted it. Hesitantly. "You keep a stash of these for all your girlfriends, whenever they sleep over?"

He crossed his arms. "No, they're Candace's. So, I can only assume *she* stashes them for all her *boyfriends* who sleep over. If any of them has ever made it that far."

His joke about his hard-nosed sister had me giggling. I poked him with the brush. "You're cruel."

"According to you and your grandmother, I'm Gregory Peck."

"I see it's also in your nature to eavesdrop." I didn't bother to hide my snide tone. I headed for the bathroom down the hall with his laughter following me.

"I guess that makes us even, now doesn't it, Sutherland?"

Chapter Three

I stepped out of the comforter and left it in a heap on the shag bathroom rug. I took a long hard look at myself in the mirror. My hair was a tangled mess and my makeup was near nonexistent, save for the mascara still stuck to my lashes. Joseph's bright blue University of Kentucky jersey made me look paler than normal too. I couldn't believe he woke to the sight of *this* monstrosity and wanted to kiss it.

Glancing at the toothbrush in my hand, I realized I'd walked away from Joseph without asking where Candace kept the toothpaste. I sighed.

"Side drawer on the right," Joseph called, as if he knew I was standing there wondering.

I yanked open the drawer and a tube of Crest 3D White slid to the front. "Thanks," I yelled over my shoulder. I squirted a good amount on the bristles and went to work on my fuzzy teeth, gawking at my appearance again in the mirror.

"You look fine, Sutherland," I heard him say.

"Oh, my gosh," I said, my mouth full of white foam. "Do you have a camera in here or something?"

"I just know you."

I finished brushing, spit, brushed again for good measure, rinsed and spit again and dropped the toothbrush on the counter. "You think you *know* me?"

"I know you well enough to know you're in there bashing yourself."

I glanced into the mirror and scowled. "No, I wasn't." But my lie only encouraged him to intervene instead of drop the subject. The door handle turned and I leapt forward to block him from entering. "Do not come in here,

Joseph," I said, peeking through the ajar door. "I'm not dressed to receive."

"Oh, cut the act, Ava Gardner."

I tried to slam the door shut, but his palm blocked it and he barreled in anyway.

"Tell me you weren't in here picking yourself apart in front of the mirror, and I'll leave."

Feeling very self-conscience about my bare legs, I yanked down the hem of his jersey. It drove me crazy that I could be so transparent. "All right. Maybe a little."

He shook his head. "This, coming from a woman who's independent, knows what she wants in life, and has worked hard enough to build her own thriving business."

"That has everything to do with my character, not my looks."

"Well, I think you're stunning."

I looked away, finding his words hard to believe. Sure, I could look in a mirror and see that I had some pleasing features. My teeth were perfectly straight and I smiled a lot. But to say I was stunning seemed a far stretch.

Joseph turned my face toward him. "Wanna know why I think you're stunning? Because you don't know you are. And that makes you the most beautiful woman in the room."

"Not if I stand in a room with Caroline. I can't hold a candle to her." I saw his eyes widen ever so slightly and his shoulders straighten as if hearing her name pin pricked something deep inside him. I regretted my words immediately. "I'm sorry. I shouldn't have said that."

"No, I'm glad you did."

"You are?"

"Yes, because it proves my point. Caroline is a very attractive woman. I'll be the first to admit it. However, she *knows* she's gorgeous, which means that's as far as her appeal goes. Skin deep. Go beneath that and there's nothing worth a second look. You, on the other hand, *can't* see how beautiful you are. There's not an ounce of conceit in you and that's what makes you a total bombshell."

A comfortable warmth spread through me and I couldn't contain my joy.

"You're smiling. So, we good here?"

"Yes."

His deep voice dropped to a husky whisper. "Good. Now, kiss me."

My body trembled with excitement and my brain went blank. He tasted of refreshing mint and something richly masculine that could only be described as Joseph. An overwhelming numbness swept over me as if this were our first kiss. Only this wasn't our first. Not even the second, third or fourth. I'd lost count after last night.

I was assuredly falling for this man. And for the first time in my life, it felt safe to do so.

"You're smiling again."

"I'm happy," I claimed, unwilling to end the kiss. I wrapped my arms around his neck and pressed my lips harder against his. All I wanted was to get closer to him.

I felt two strong hands cup my bottom. Callouses scraped against the satin of my panties as he lifted and hiked my legs around his waist. He crushed me against the open bathroom door and it gave way. Swinging back on its hinges, it slammed into the rigid stopper behind it. The sudden jarring clacked our teeth together.

"Ow!" we both exclaimed simultaneously, then laughed.

"Are you okay?" Joseph asked.

I ran my tongue across my front teeth to make certain I hadn't chipped them. "Yeah, I'm good. You?"

I watched him do the same and I felt my stomach somersault at the sight of his tongue moving so skillfully. "All good here too."

"Who knew kissing could be so dangerous."

He laughed at my joke and I loved him for it.

"Next time we kiss," he said, reaching above my head and knocking, "I'll have to remember to utilize a wall, not a door."

"More 'next times,' huh? You're good at planning those."

"So, I've been told." He snickered and staked his thumbs in his front pockets. He leaned against the bathroom vanity, contemplating something. "You know...you're actually the first girl I enjoy having 'next times' with. I find myself looking forward to them."

"Is that so?"

"Mmm-hmm. It is." He snagged my hand and pulled me to him. "And speaking of next time...you are so wearing this jersey again." He brushed my hair back and revealed the number on the front, his eyes full of lust. Full of promise. "Thirty-three is definitely my lucky number."

I slowly leaned forward and kissed him one last time to savor this moment. I drew in a long breath and released it. "Now get out, so I can get my shower."

Another chuckle shook his body. "Yes, ma'am. Need any help?"

I touched his prickly cheek. "I think I got it. Left is hot. Right is cold."

He cleared his throat and pushed himself from the vanity. "Yeah, I've got to get out of here before I need another one."

"Another shower?"

He stepped into the hall and respired heavily. "I don't think the first one was cold enough."

Chapter Four

I stood in the shower, letting the hot water cascade down my back. Steam filled the bathroom as happiness filled my heart. It had been a long time since I'd felt so elated, this high on life. It was almost as good as the day I'd opened my coffee shop, but without all the stress of its potential failure.

Normally by now, I'd be second guessing the direction of this new relationship because things were going too well. I'd fret about how long it would last, almost betting against myself. Being a serial, ruined-relationship survivor does that to a person.

But with Joseph, I didn't feel so cynical. I felt confident in the days ahead and looked forward to having him involved in every aspect of my life. He was good for me and it seemed, I was good for him.

Though we came from different worlds, in time our lives had meshed. My independence and lack of self-absorption was as much medicine for him as his honest and sincere camaraderie was for me. My heart felt whole again. Stitched back together by the tender thread of Joseph's casual yet notable existence.

Deep down, I knew we were perfect for each other and nothing could come between us. Not even Caroline.

"Hey, Jamie."

His deep voice broke through the happy fog of my roving thoughts. I peered out of the shower curtain and projected my voice so he could hear me. "Yes?"

"Candace made breakfast for us. You got time to stay?"

"Sure."

"Everything's okay at the coffee shop?"

I remembered I'd told Joseph I needed to call in, even though I hadn't. "Oh, yeah. Things are fine. I can stay."

"Perfect. I'll wait for you."

"I'll just be a minute." I squirted shampoo in my hand and lathered up. I washed my hair and body as quickly as I could. I dried off and stepped out of the shower. The mound of blankets lay on the bath mat. *Crap. I forgot to bring in my clothes with me.*

There wasn't much chance Joseph hadn't waited for me, but I wished this once he would've gone on down to breakfast. I wrapped a fluffy mint green bath towel around my body and laid my lips against the bathroom door.

"Joseph?"

"Forgot something, didn't you?"

I tipped my head back and sighed, squirming my toes into the bath rug. "Yes…"

"I've got your clothes right here."

I cracked the door open and peeked through. Joseph stood, casually leaning against the frame, with my clothes neatly folded on his palm. "Here you go."

"Thanks." I snatched them out of his hand and ripped the towel from my body, throwing it at him. I saw it wrap around his grinning face before I slammed the door.

"So not fair, Sutherland."

I giggled and turned the lock for good measure.

I dressed as fast as I could and ran my fingers through my damp hair. I didn't dare look in the mirror again for fear Joseph would call me out. When I stepped out of the bathroom, he lunged at me and pulled me into his arms.

"You think you're something else, don't you?" Joseph said huskily. He tickled my ribs to underscore his point. I wriggled out of his arms, our laughter knitting us together like a fuzzy, warm sweater. Yes, we were a great pair.

His hand clasped mine and he led me down the hall toward the kitchen, his smile still beaming.

"I think I heard my other sister downstairs. Her name's Miranda. You'll like her. She's not as rude as Candace, but she's twice as tough."

I trotted down the steps with Joseph leading the way. To my surprise, he stopped at the base of the staircase, keeping me one step higher. I was eye level with his handsome face and a tremor of anticipation raced through me as he blocked my path. His long arms braced the wall at one side of me and the railing at the other.

"Don't be nervous. Miranda's harmless."

I pretended to be nonchalant. "Okay."

"I don't want you to feel overwhelmed."

"Why would I feel overwhelmed? I've already met Candace."

"Yeah, but I should warn you. Candace is in a mood."

"Because of me?" I hated to think I'd ticked her off by spending the night with her brother.

"Nah, she just gets this way every so often and for no good reason. Just do what I do. Ignore her."

My stomach knotted up. If Candace was in a mood, I worried what she might have said about me to Miranda. It would be two against one, and I sucked at contact sports.

"Hey," he soothed. "Don't let Candace scare you. Trust me, her bark is worse than her bite."

I tried to shake off my nerves and pep talked my wary self from inside the batter's box. "Right. Okay. I can do this."

His eyes shimmered like blue diamonds. "I know you can." He draped his arm around my shoulder and pulled me off the step. Tugging me close against his side, we walked together into the kitchen where his two sisters sat at the table.

A hush came over them as we made our entrance, conjoined as if we'd been close all our lives. With the peculiar looks we received, I felt safer near him.

"Miranda, this is Jamie," Joseph blurted out. "Jamie, Miranda."

Miranda exchanged a surprised smile with Candace. I assumed she expected Caroline to accompany her brother.

"Please, call me Randi." She stood to shake my hand across the table. "It's nice to meet you."

I extended my hand as well and, like Candace, calluses scraped against my soft palm. I tried not to get hung up on the fact that we came from totally different worlds. I only hoped she didn't think less of me because my hands lacked the feel of rough sandpaper.

"Sit, please. Make yourself at home." Miranda gestured toward an open seat.

Joseph and I chose the pair of chairs next to each other and sat down. I noticed the old fashioned china and silverware and realized they were the same ones used to set the table in the woods last night. Maybe that's why she was in a mood. Her brother had "borrowed" them, just like he had the Christmas lights.

"Can I get you some coffee?" Miranda asked.

I dismissed my thoughts and played innocent. "Yes, please."

"Me too, Sis," Joseph called over his shoulder.

As Miranda rounded the table to get the coffee pot from the counter, I glanced in Candace's direction. "And I appreciate you letting me stay last night."

"It's no trouble at all. You're welcome to stay anytime."

Okay, that was a good sign. It seemed Candace's mood was not because of me. And it couldn't have been from Miranda since all was well between them when we entered. That left only Joseph.

"So, what were you two doing in the woods so late?"

Oh, there it is. The bait. I squirmed in my seat and made myself busy. I took the napkin from under my place setting and laid it across my lap. I wondered how Joseph was going to break the news to her.

"Yeah, about that," he began tentatively as Miranda poured coffee in both our cups.

"Save it, Joey. I already know what you did. And you better make sure those lights come down—today—or I'll kick your ass."

Miranda chuckled as she sat back down. "What lights is she talking about, Joseph?"

He rolled his eyes, but before he could answer Miranda, Candace out spoke him. "My Christmas lights. My china. *And* my brand new propane heater that Dad bought me. All carted off to his stupid treehouse down by the lake."

I watched Miranda as she scooped a spoonful of scrambled eggs onto her plate, trying to gauge her reaction to Candace's gripe session. "What was all that stuff for?"

Joseph first looked at me and smiled, as if he were recalling the wonderful night we had together, and then back at Randi. "I wanted to surprise Jamie with a special evening. Dinner for two at the place where we first got to know each other. But I wanted to make it something she'd never forget. Thus, the lights."

As the food made its way around the table, I filled my plate, taking in the two sisters' reactions. Miranda smiled with pride at her little brother, while Candace glared at him. I quickly determined that Randi often found delight in the off-the-wall things her little brother did, while Candace was not so approving. I figured it had a lot to do with the age difference.

Randi was much older, in her early forties, putting her as the sibling who had helped to raise the younger ones of the family. A mother hen. While Candace, on the other hand, was closer to Joseph's age and probably had to compete with him all her life. Given he was the only son, I imagined he was a momma's boy and could do no wrong, leaving Candace resentful growing up. It was obvious her bitterness carried over in her adult years.

"Call me curious, Jamie," Miranda said as she spread her toast with jelly. "But what did my little brother make for dinner?"

I peppered my hash browns and passed the shaker to Joseph, meeting his gaze again. "Pizza. Carry out."

Candace scoffed. "Real romantic there, Joey."

"Hey, I was limited in my choices given the weather. Cut me some slack."

Miranda chimed in and I was glad for it. I felt bad that Joseph was taking some serious heat for something he'd done for me. "Don't you think you're overreacting a little, Candace? I think what he did is cute."

Candace piled her plate with bacon. "Cute? I don't think so. He comes to my house on Wednesday, claiming he's here to help me get things done on the farm, when all the while he's stealing my stuff. He's a regular con artist."

"A romantic con artist it seems," Randi insisted.

"You'd feel differently if he used *your* china and *your* Christmas lights."

"I would've used Randi's, but they're all packed." Joseph elbowed me gently, gaining my attention. He didn't look at all concerned with Candace's protests. I, on the other hand, was still trying to figure out my place in this discussion and what was appropriate for me to say on Joseph's behalf, should I speak at all. "Randi's moving out west."

"Oh, how exciting," I said, hoping to direct the conversation elsewhere.

"Yeah it is pretty cool. Spencer's work is transferring him to Colorado, and I'll be that much closer to my rescued 'stangs. My daughter, Evelyn's not too happy about it, but the twins are. Henry and Hunter are like their father. Up for an adventure with no ties to hold them down."

"How old is Evelyn?" I asked, eating my eggs first.

"She's fifteen, so she's pretty upset about leaving her high school and friends behind. But she's a tough girl. She'll adjust soon enough. I've heard they have a great school system out there."

"Speaking of relocating, Joey," Candace intervened. "I assume you'll be relocating my Christmas lights from your treehouse to my house—today?"

"Yeeees, Candace," Joseph droned. "I'll even do one better. I'll cut down a pine tree and set it up in your living room, lights and all. How's that sound?"

Candace nibbled on her toast, pondering his offer. "Fine. But no mistletoe. You hang that crap up, I'm tearing it down."

I nearly choked on my food hearing Candace be so direct and objectionable at the breakfast table. It's no wonder the woman was single. I imagined Joseph was the only man alive who could deal with her prickly personality.

"Cross my heart, Ms. Scrooge." He gave her shoulder a mild shove. "See? Little brother always takes care of you."

"Shut up and eat." Candace glanced at Miranda "And wipe that smile off your face. Don't encourage him."

Miranda kept smiling despite her sister's reprimand. "I don't think I'm the one encouraging him."

All eyes, even Joseph's, landed on me.

The weight of their stares caught me off guard. It was time for me to speak and God only knows how I found the words. "For what it's worth, I can't take credit for any of Joseph's behavior, good or bad. But I did appreciate the lengths he went to surprise me with such a magical evening. No man has ever done that for me. And your lights and china were beautiful, Candace."

"He's never done that for anyone," Randi added. "Not even Caroline."

Candace cringed, setting her fork down as if the mere mention of Joseph's ex ruined her appetite. "Really? Did you have to mention *her* name at my table?"

"Admit it. It's nice to see Joseph go the extra mile for someone other than—"

"I got it," Candace interrupted. "And, yes, I'm super thrilled my brother has finally come to his senses and found someone I can actually get along with. So there. I said it. I approve my brother's choice of…"

Candace stopped and looked to Joseph for assistance.

I swallowed hard, wondering how he'd publically acknowledge me. I dabbed my napkin at the corner of my mouth and waited.

"Girlfriend," Joseph finally stated matter-of-factly. "If that's okay with Jamie."

The term echoed in my head.

Girlfriend.

I drew in a deep breath, unprepared for the way Joseph punted the ball to my side of the field. *Girlfriend.*

Again, I heard it rattle around in my brain, though it did little to ease the weight of everyone's stare. I tried to block them all out. How *did* I feel about being his girlfriend?

I made him laugh on a regular basis and he made me feel wanted and loved. So, at the present, I felt pretty darn good about it. I wanted to rejoice in the term he referred to me, but now wasn't the time to be sappy.

Recollections of the night we first kissed came to mind and how we both stumbled on the right words to call what we planned a "date." Almost verbatim, I chose the same phrase I said then and lifted my coffee cup in a toast. "I suppose we couldn't dodge this bullet, if we tried."

He picked up his cup and clinked it with mine. His free hand came up to my cheek and he leaned forward to kiss me. I froze, feeling the sweet demand of this man's impulsive behavior. I almost forgot his sisters were still in the room.

"Okay. Now I'm officially grossed out." Candace pushed her chair out and removed herself from the table to eat in the living room.

Joseph's rumbling laughter tickled me, though I was still concerned that Candace was disgusted with me as well. I hated to think she cared for me as little as she had cared for Caroline.

To my surprise, she gave me a reassuring wink as she exited down the hall. "Remember Joey. No mistletoe or I'll shove it where the sun doesn't shine."

Chapter Five

After breakfast, Joseph and I gathered our belongings from upstairs. I made sure both beds were made, the bathroom towels hung up, and the rooms were in better condition than I found them. There was no way I'd do anything to bring the wrath of Candace down upon me.

I checked my cell for any missed calls. No one had called me from the coffee shop. No news is good news, I always say. I shoved my cell in my purse and slipped into my winter coat and hat. If I stayed to help Joseph, I wouldn't have to go home soon. I opened my bedroom door and met Joseph in his Carhartt as he came out of his room. A huge smile radiated on his lips. His arms immediately enveloped me.

"You got everything?"

I patted my coat and purse strap. "I think so."

"Good." He laid his forehead on mine and brushed the tip of his nose along my cheek, closing his eyes. "I've had so much fun."

"Joey! You're burning daylight! Those Christmas lights aren't going to take themselves down!"

Candace's voice resounded from the first floor, interrupting the kiss Joseph was about to initiate. He straightened his back and calmly lifted his index finger. "Excuse me a minute." Leaning away from me, he averted his face over his shoulder. "I'm on it, Candace! Quit yer bitchin'. I'm doing you a favor!"

I laid my hand across my mouth to keep from laughing. At their ages, it was quite comical to hear them bicker like little kids. When he angled himself back into our embrace, he caught sight of my amusement.

"What?"

"Nothing," I insisted, ushering him down the hall. "Come on, we need to get those lights down before she has a conniption."

"No, there's no *we*."

"Yes, I'm helping you take them down."

At the top of the stairs, he took hold of both my hands. "I appreciate you wanting to, but this is my responsibility. Besides, there's no way I'm letting you climb a ladder again."

He was right. Ladders and I didn't get along.

"I'll tell you what," he proposed as he descended the steps with me in tow. "I'll drop you off at your grandmother's so you can spend some time with her while I *tend to my chores*." He punctuated the last four words with his fingers crooked in quotations. "And when I'm finished, I'll pick you both up. We'll go to dinner or something."

We stopped at the bottom of the staircase and I had to lift my chin to meet his eyes. "I don't feel comfortable leaving you to climb a tree and—"

"I'll be fine. This ain't my first rodeo."

I planted my hands on my hips. "What if you fall?"

"I'll call you."

His nonchalance hardly humored me. "I'm serious, Joseph."

"So am I," he said, cupping my face. "I'll be fine."

I could do nothing but let him kiss me. He could easily convince me of anything with those lips. I swear the man could talk me into skydiving over a cactus field.

After our kiss, he yelled to Candace to let her know where we were going and we made our way to his truck. Like a gentleman, he opened the door for me and helped me climb inside. As I buckled myself in, I relished the lasting scent of his cologne infused in the vehicle's upholstery.

He shut the door, unaware of my delight over his compelling manly aroma. He rounded the front with a swagger only Joseph could pull off and climbed into the driver's seat. Clicking his seat belt, he gave me a look that would stop a woman's heart.

"You ready?"

I cleared my throat, shaking the shivers from my spine. "Yep." Inwardly, I wondered what I'd done to deserve him. After countless heartbreaks, had I finally found the one?

"Paris, Kentucky, right? That's where your grandmother lives?"

"Yes. Right off Duncan Avenue."

He thought for a quick second and shook his head "Gosh, I haven't been to Paris in years, but I know exactly where it's at." He turned the key and fired up the engine. The vehicle seemed to rumble with as much testosterone as its driver. The two were a perfect fit. Popping the clutch, the 4-wheel-drive diesel lunged forward. Joseph spun the steering wheel, sending the truck into a spin in Candace's gravel drive.

My hands immediately braced against the door and seat. My body leaned into the turn driven there by momentum. Joseph laughed as we tore down the laneway. "Hang on!"

I squealed as I was thrown back against the seat. "Candace is going to kill you."

"I know," he said, looking over his shoulder out the back window. I glanced over my shoulder too to see whether Candace was standing there shaking her fist at us. She wasn't thankfully, but I could just imagine her reaction when she finds out Joseph had thrown gravel all over her front lawn.

Dust billowed behind us as we sped along. I shook my head and laughed. Joseph enjoyed poking the bear as much as Candace did, only he did it with actions instead of words. He was an instigator from the word go. I wondered if he and Candace would ever grow up.

We passed beneath the wrought iron *Pride and Joy* sign, and Joseph shifted again. The truck bounced from the gravel onto the pavement. If not for my seat belt, I'd have hit my head on the cab roof.

Joseph laughed at me and shifted gears. The truck accelerated and we roared down the road. "Fun, isn't it?"

Good grief. Boys and their toys.

"Tell me that wasn't fun, Jamie." He glanced at me, taking his eyes off the road momentarily, willing me to agree with him. "It's even more fun in a hay field."

"*Not* Candace's hayfield...."

Joseph's hearty laughter filled the cab. "No, not Candace's. I know better than that. But I have been known to rip up Randi's field. Well, before I sold it to her anyway."

"You think Randi will sell the property back to you? I mean with her moving out west, she'll have to give up her home here, won't she?"

His wrist rested casually on the steering wheel as he spoke. "I imagine. I told her if she was ever ready to sell, I'm her man."

I thought about how selfish Caroline must have been to even think of asking Joseph to sell his plot of land, so he could move closer to her. The fact that she didn't appreciate his sacrifices, made me dislike her even more. How could she live with herself?

I turned and looked out the window so Joseph couldn't see the grimace on my face. I pushed her out of my mind. As I watched the blackboard fence speed by, I forced myself to think of pleasant things, like Joseph's strong arms and savory lips.

"You know, I was thinking," Joseph said, interrupting my reverie. "This has been the first time I've ever had a girl over at my family's place and it not be uncomfortable."

Well. How about that? Chalk one up for Jamie. *Nada* for the she-devil.

"I think Candace and Randi really like you."

"You think so?" I hoped so. I wanted their approval badly, and I believed I may have succeeded. It was difficult though to tell whether they were just relieved he moved on from Caroline or if they truly liked me.

"Oh, yeah, definitely. Trust me. You'd know if Candace didn't approve."

I laughed at the dig on his sister. She was a lot like *my* sister—headstrong, opinionated, and unreserved. Maybe that's why I felt more inclined to want her favor than Miranda's. "I'm glad I didn't embarrass you."

"Embarrass me?" He downshifted and slowed into the turn onto I-75, before looking my way. "Heck, no. You were great. Really. It was nice having you with me. It's weird actually being able to say that and mean it."

Hearing Joseph talk about me with such high regard never got old. I soared every time he whistled at me, praised the look of my legs, or remarked about how good I kissed.

"Call me crazy, Sutherland, but I could get used to this."

"What?"

"You and me. Together. All the time." He settled into the cushion of the truck seat. "I used to think my friends were nuts for trapping themselves in serious relationships. I could never understand why anyone would want to settle down with one person for *their whole life*. To me, that was ludicrous."

I swallowed hard, listening to Joseph bare his soul. Was this that pivotal moment just before my world came crashing down? That split second pause just before the rug was jerked from under me? I wasn't certain I was prepared for this because I already allowed myself to dream that I'd found the one person I could settle down with. My breath hitched in my throat while I waited for the other shoe to fall.

Joseph reached for my hand. "And then you came along."

Chapter Six

The blue in Joseph's eyes shocked me as he turned to deliver that line. Maybe it was the sunlight streaming through the windshield that made them so brilliant, but all I saw was a cerulean blue sky over a picturesque Montana afternoon with a picnic blanket and Joseph sprawled next to me, feeding me chocolate covered strawberries. My perfect world.

"You're so different from all the other women I've met. For one, you've never thrown yourself at me." He chuckled. "In fact, you always seem to resist me."

How he thought that was beyond me. The way I recalled it, all he had to do was look at me and I was putty.

"I like that you make me work for it, Sutherland."

"You do, huh?"

He nodded reminiscently. "Yeah. That's why I can't stop thinking about you. I like knowing that at any minute, I could say or do the wrong thing and possibly lose you—which for the record, is the last thing I want to do. But with you, comes this challenge. That maybe for the first time in my life, I might fall in love with someone who may not fall in love with me. Do you understand what I'm getting at?"

Actually, I didn't. I wanted to assume I knew, but because of my past boyfriends who said one thing and did another, I couldn't begin to fathom what he really meant.

I watched him run his hand over his scruffy jaw. The lines on his face told me he struggled to find the right words. I couldn't help him this time. I had my own relationship issues.

"What I mean is," he finally said, taking hold of the steering wheel with both hands, "I like being with someone who's impossible to take advantage of."

Obviously, he did not know me. "Oh, it's been done."

"No, I get that—your past and all. But it's impossible...for *me*. I can't begin to imagine taking advantage of you or your friendship because it means so much. I know we've only known each other a few weeks, but it's been the best few weeks of my life."

He reached over and laid his hand on mine. The heat from his touch warmed me. I flipped my hand over beneath his and interlaced our fingers. "Mine too."

The strength of his grasp soothed me in ways he couldn't possibly understand. Being a man who'd never felt the gut-wrenching, near strangling choke hold of love before, he couldn't know what it felt like to be head-over-heels with someone who'd eventually rip the rug out from under you and tear your heart out in one fail swoop. I'd been the recipient of so many BS lines about finding their soul mate that I'd always been leery of men who seemingly spoke from the heart.

But Joseph was different. Somehow, he had a way of making me feel like he wasn't just saying all these things for the sake of an ulterior motive.

I looked down at our conjoined hands. You couldn't even see mine beneath the breadth of his. Only my fingertips resting between each manly knuckle. It was a weird fetish, but I loved large, masculine hands. His, by far, were construction worker's hands; callused, banged up, and brawny. Nothing about his hands said *I sit at a computer desk for a living*. And yet this macho, bone-crushing, man hand held mine with delicate care.

What made it even more special was knowing he felt just as comfortable holding hands. Though it was an unpretentious public display of affection, it still had an audaciousness about it that proclaimed 'I'm taken. Don't even try to hit on me.'

I loved holding his hand, but we'd both gone deathly silent. I didn't want him to suddenly feel awkward and let go. I spoke to lighten the mood. "So, you said you'd hadn't been to Paris in years. What took you there?"

Joseph grinned. "Our band played at Varden's all the time on weekends. I think it's called the Grey Goose now."

"Oh, yeah. On Main Street."

"Yep, that's the one."

I thought back to my college days when everyone else was out with their boyfriends and I was spending the weekend with Grandma, sipping hot tea, assembling jigsaw puzzles and learning how to crochet. I remembered our nights spent on her back patio, listening to the faint sound of a rock band and 'chewing the cud' as she liked to call our gab sessions. "I probably was listening to you guys and didn't even know it."

"You were at Varden's?"

"Not when you played, 'cause I would've surely recognized you. But I used to sit on my grandmother's patio and hear music coming from across town. Like I said, I might have heard you playing there."

"Well, it's probably better you didn't know me then. I was your typical lead singer, charming all the groupies hanging around the stage mic."

"How'd Caroline feel about that?"

He laughed heartily. "One time we were playing there, and I had a few too many. At a song change, I pointed to some blonde in the crowd who I thought was Caroline and I said 'this one's for *you*, babe.' She was not happy."

Joseph drawled out the 'not.' Dang, I wish I'd been there to see Caroline's face.

"Especially since the chick I called out bought the band a round of beers. Luckily, though, my drummer saved my butt that night. He told Caroline he had the hots for the blonde and the dedication came from him. Which wasn't a stretch from the truth since he took her home that night. But without him, I wouldn't have had a ride home. Caroline was ready to leave me behind at two in the morning."

"I'm sure some other girl in the bar would've taken you home."

"Yeah, well. No one worth losing your dignity over." He gave my hand a squeeze and shot me a dazzling smile. "Now, if you'd been there, I would've let *you* drive me home."

"Who says I would've offered?"

"Ouch, Sutherland."

I loved that we could joke around and cut each other up without fearing the other might take offense. We often laughed together, and in my mind, I memorized that sound. Everything about Joseph's laughter was noteworthy. The way his whole body shook. The way his beautiful, straight teeth gleamed behind perfect, kissable lips. The way his eyes sparkled like sunlight over a rippling river.

We spent the rest of the ride to my grandmother's house pointing out how much things had changed from when we were younger. It wasn't so astonishing for me since I visited Grandma on a regular basis and had seen the modifications to the quaint little town over time. But we shared stories of places we recalled as teens. I especially enjoyed Joseph's recollections of where he went on his first date and the exact spot he stole his first kiss, which thankfully didn't involve Caroline.

As we passed the Grey Goose and finally turned a few corners onto Duncan Avenue, I directed Joseph down the little country lane bordered with tall, old oak trees. In the middle of summer, this historic street was a dazzling display of colorful perennials, lush green lawns, and magnificent shade trees embellishing some of the most charming Queen Anne style houses in Paris, Kentucky.

"Right here," I pointed. "This is it."

He pulled the truck in the drive, and I regarded my grandmother's Folk Victorian home. The L-shaped, two-story cottage hugged a semi-spacious porch adorned with fanciful white spindles, posts, railings, and angle braces. The bluish gray siding offset the whimsical trimmings and scalloped bargeboards along the gables of the house.

"Wow, what a neat place," Joseph remarked as he killed the engine. "I bet you loved coming here when you were little."

"Still do." I glanced at the upper, front window where I'd room on certain occasions. A memory washed over me of sitting there on the cushioned dormer bench on breezy summer afternoons with a romance novel and a cup of coffee.

Without hesitation, Joseph opened his truck door and got out, his gaze still fixed on my grandmother's house. I opened my door, and he quickly rounded the truck and assisted me to the ground with a smile. "Are you nervous?"

I furrowed my brow. "Why would I be?"

"Because you're introducing me to one of your family members. I don't know much about your past boyfriends, except that the majority of them were assholes. I imagine you probably regretted bringing them around."

"*All* of them were assholes and huge regrets. But I don't think you have anything to worry about in that department. My grandmother's going to love you."

"'Cause of my hair, right? How's it look?" He smoothed his sexy, unruly lock away from his forehead with his fingers and struck a GQ pose.

I elbowed him as I passed by. "You look fine, Fonzarelli."

He chuckled and took my hand. We climbed the porch steps together. A nostalgic smell of weathered wood and wet pine hit me. It made me smile knowing Grandma still applied a layer of pine needles as mulch around her landscaping bushes. Being a citizen of the Depression, she reused common items for multiple purposes. It was a habit impossible for her to break.

I rang the doorbell and crossed my arms behind my back. Rocking back on my heels, I looked at Joseph standing beside me.

"You are nervous, aren't you?"

I sighed. "Okay, maybe a little."

He wrapped his left arm around my shoulders and tugged me close. "Don't worry, I promise I won't embarrass you. I'll be on my best behavior. Scouts honor."

I leaned into his hug and tried to steal every ounce of confidence from him. I loved how calm and collected he was all the time. He made life, with all its trials and tribulations, look so easy. Given Grandma was one of the most important persons in my life, I wanted to finally make a good impression. I wanted to prove that Jamett Penelope Sutherland could actually pick a quality boyfriend and keep him.

After what seemed like five whole minutes, my grandmother's voice sounded through the door. "Who is it?"

Relieved she remembered to check before letting a visitor enter her home, I took a step forward so she could hear me. "It's me, Grandma. Jamie."

"Jamie?" she asked, cracking the door open. Her blessed face lit up when she saw me smiling back at her through the old screen door. "Come in, come in. What a wonderful surprise."

Joseph held the screen door open and ushered me in first. I held out my arms and embraced my grandmother carefully. I felt her scoliotic spine with its frail, boney protrusions, and I couldn't help but wonder why she'd lost so much weight over the last year. She always assured me it was just old age, but in the back of my mind, I worried it might be more.

"You said you'd visit soon, but I didn't know you meant today. Or did we make plans? I may have forgotten."

"No, Grandma. You're fine. I didn't say anything about coming over today." I looked at Joseph, including him. "We just decided to visit."

I slipped my arm around his, emphasizing the 'we' part. "Grandma, this is Joseph Scarbrough."

Chapter Seven

Grandma's eyes lifted toward Joseph, and I could see her measuring him up. "Jamie's told me a lot about you, Joseph."

He took her outstretched hand, sandwiching hers between both of his in a gentle grasp. "All good things, I hope."

He gave her that charming boy-next-door smile, and I knew Grandma was as taken with him as I'd been the first day I met him. Lucky for Grandma, though, he was fully dressed. I imagined she'd have suffered cardiac arrest, if she'd seen him wearing nothing but a towel and a smile.

I looked down and saw she had yet to let go of Joseph's hand. He didn't seem to mind and kept the conversation going.

"You have a lovely home here, ma'am. So much character and warmth. I feel right at home."

I couldn't agree more. Inside was an eclectic combination of mahogany hardwood floors, high ceilings, and decorative crown molding. Each inner door was solid wood and arched, complete with crystal knobs and skeleton keys, a veritable old-world fantasy realm for the young at heart.

Grandmother blushed at his compliment. "Well, I do try to keep things tidy. A clean house is a happy house, I always say." She patted his hand with as much fervor as her arthritic hands could handle. "Come, sit down. How about some coffee?"

"I would love to, ma'am, but I have some work to do on my sister's farm in Lexington."

"Oh, that's too bad." Grandma's puckered her lips in disappointment.

I touched her arm. "I'm going to stay though."

"Yes, Jamie's going to stay here with you while I finish up, and then later this evening, I'd love to take you both out to dinner."

Joseph's voice was deep and soothing. Grandma stood there staring at him as if he was the second coming. He gave her hand—still tucked in his—a little squeeze. "It would be an honor."

A small nervous laugh came out of my blushing grandmother as her hand came to rest on her bosom. "Oh, how sweet of you, dear." She looked at me and spoke out of the side of her mouth. "Hang on to this one, child. He's a keeper."

Joseph leaned toward my grandmother and looked right at me. "I keep trying to tell her that, but you know Jamie. She's hard to convince."

She winked at him in the most flirtatious way. "I'll put in a good word for you."

"That's most generous of you, ma'am."

"Please," Grandma insisted. "Call me Rose."

I stood astounded at the way my grandmother gushed over Joseph. She'd always been a good judge of character, so I derived from her blatant swooning that I had nothing to worry about where Joseph was concerned. This was good. Very good.

"All right, dear, you shuffle off to your sister's and get your work finished and Jamie and I will catch up over coffee." She finally let go of his hand, but I could tell she would have rather not. "Do you have a hat? You need a hat, Joseph. It's cold out there."

I smiled as she fretted over him. As a child, it was the one thing she fussed about whenever we went outside—to make sure we wore a hat over our ears and never sat on the ground with an "R" in the month. Her blood thinner medication made her cold all the time now, so her nagging about dressing warmly had escalated, even in mild temperatures.

Joseph reassured her he had one in the truck and would put it on just for her. I was grateful he went the extra mile to ease her mind. I supposed he learned how to with a house full of women.

He reached for my hand and pulled me toward the door. "I'll be back to pick you gals up around five-thirty." He hugged me and whispered in my ear. "How'd I do?"

I gave him a huge smile and replied to him in code. "Five-thirty is *perfect*. I couldn't ask for a better time."

"Actually, five would be better," Grandma interjected, "if we want to beat the Saturday night dinner crowd."

Joseph gave me smile, knowing my grandmother didn't comprehend my cryptic message. "I'll do my best, ma'am."

"Rose," she corrected, shooing him out the door. "And don't forget that hat."

I watched Joseph jog down the steps with a skip to his swagger. Grandmother also watched him like a hawk, and I had to smile at her overzealous behavior. When he reached his truck, he opened the back door, pulled out an old knit cap and held it up for Grandma's sake before pulling it over his head. I confess I didn't believe he had a cap in his truck, but I enjoyed the fact that his promise wasn't just a bunch of mollifying gibberish.

Joseph was definitely a keeper.

As he climbed in the cab and pulled away, my grandmother closed the door with a satisfied look on her face. "He's a nice boy."

It cracked me up that she referred to Joseph, a grown man in his thirties, as a boy. "Yes, he is."

"That's a big truck he's got. Will we be going to dinner in that?"

I realized she was probably worried over the high climb. "I'll help you get up in there."

She scoffed. "All one hundred pounds of you? I'd like to see that. But I'm betting your Joseph can hoist me up. A working man always has a strong back." She shook her head as she shuffled down the hall to the kitchen. "He's going to need it."

I followed her, eager to have coffee with my Grandma. "We'll get you in safe and sound."

"I'm not so worried about getting in as I am falling out. I don't need a broken hip."

I patted her gently on the shoulder. "Joseph won't let you fall."

"Speaking of falling," she added, "I can see why you're so taken with him. He's quite the looker."

There was that outdated vernacular again. "Yeah, he's a good looking man. Hard to believe he's into me."

"Oh, you shush." She flapped one hand at me as I retrieved two coffee cups from her kitchen cupboard. "You're a beautiful young lady and any man would be lucky to court you."

"You're family, Grandma. You're supposed to say that."

"Pour that coffee and button your lip."

I obeyed my Grandma, taking particular notice of how slowly she eased into the kitchen chair. "Your arthritis acting up again?"

"This damn weather. I'd be better off living in Florida. You know, your mom and dad are thinking about moving there."

I recalled their conversation at Thanksgiving. "I heard they already found a condo in Destin. Some gated community thing."

"That's what they say...."

I detected a tinge of insinuation in Grandma's voice. "You thinking about moving there, too?" I kept my eyes on her as I sat down across the table from her. Her lips pursed and her eyes blinked rapidly. She suddenly seemed anxious.

"I'm giving it thought. Like your mom said, it would be good for me. And better for them."

"Better for them? How?"

"Well, I'm no spring chicken, Jamie. There's a lot of things I can't do anymore and it's only getting worse as time goes on." She rubbed her hands together, easing the ache in her fingers.

"What do you need done at this house? I can help you. Just tell me. Housework? Vacuuming? I can come down once a week and do all that for you."

Again she waved me off. "You're not coming all the way down here and cleaning for me. You've got your business, and you don't need to waste gas money making the drive from Cinci just to scrub my floors. That's silly."

"Grandma," I said, laying my hand over hers. "I wouldn't mind at all."

"I know you wouldn't, dear, but I would. Besides, it's only a matter of time before this heart stops ticking."

"Don't talk like that."

"Jamie, it's true. I'm eighty-six years old and it's bound to happen sooner rather than later. If I moved to Florida with your mom and dad, I wouldn't be a nuisance for everyone."

"You're *not* a nuisance."

"I am when the closest family member is two hours away. What would happen if I fell and I couldn't get to a phone?"

"Okay, so we'll sign you up for that Life Alert thingy." My mind was spinning. I could hardly fathom my grandmother living in Florida, and I sure as heck didn't like the idea of having to fork out airfare every time I wanted to see her. Now *that* would be silly. Sure, it wasn't all that convenient from Cinci to Paris, but at least it would be more cost efficient than flying to and from the Gulf Coast. Money aside, there'd be no more 'just stopping in on a whim,' if she moved south. I could kiss my close relationship with my grandmother goodbye. I knew I wouldn't be able to afford a plane ticket every week.

"I'm not plopping money into Life Alert's pockets. That money belongs to you grandkids and whoever is left taking care of me."

"Grandma...." All this talk about broken hips, heart attacks, and nursing homes knocked the wind right out of my sails, as Grandma would say.

"And if by some chance I *do* end up in a nursing home, I need to get out from under this deed. Your grandfather built this house and the last thing I want is to hand it over to the government. They took enough from him in the war."

"What? You'd sell the house too?"

Grandma lifted her cup to her lips and took a sip. "I can't move it with me, Jamie. I have to sell it."

"To who?"

"To whoever the hell wants it."

I lifted my palms in surprise. "You can't just sell to anybody." Recollections of Miranda talking to Joseph about his part of the farm came to mind. "You have to keep it in the family."

"I'm the last of my siblings, Jamie. And your mother and father at their age don't want it, and your sister sure as heck doesn't need another mortgage when she's got a husband and a good life in D.C."

"What about me? I'll buy it." I said the words before I really thought about what it would take to purchase it.

"Jamie, be realistic. You can't afford to buy this house when you've already put everything into your coffee shop business. That means too much to you to let it go under. I'll not hear of it."

I ignored her crooked finger pointing at me. "Actually, Grandma, I have a nice little nest egg saved up *because* of that business. I could very well buy this house with cash and be just fine."

"You do that and it'll piss me off," Grandma snapped.

I stuffed my laughter down my throat. Hearing my little old grandmother curse sounded comical to my ears—until I really looked at her and realized she was serious. I calmed my voice to a low, soothing tone. "I'm sorry, Grandma. I didn't mean to upset you."

The harsh lines of Grandma's face softened. "I know, honey. But you have to understand how hard it's been for me to get to this point. In a perfect world, I'd live here until the day the good Lord calls me home, but we both know that's unrealistic." Her trembling hands cupped her coffee mug and her eyes stared at the steam rising from the brim. "It's for the best that I move in with your parents where they can keep an eye on me. Besides, my memory is isn't what it used to be and some days I can't remember if I took my medicine or not. Your mother could monitor that for me."

I couldn't argue with her there. I'd noticed her memory slipping from time to time, but hated to bring it up. I took a long sip of coffee and let the idea of Grandma moving settle in. Convincing her to stay in Kentucky would only be for my benefit, so I had to try to look at the situation from her perspective.

"Seems your mind is made up, huh?"

Grandma regarded me with a grave look. "It is."

I took a long look around me. The antique china hutch that displayed all the mismatched dishes and cups Grandma had bought at yard sales, the assorted crocks and metal cooking utensils that sat above her cabinets, the lacey curtains she'd had since her wedding day hanging at every window, hand-made quilts and afghans draped over nearly every chair—they were all things as dear to her as they were to me.

"How are you going to ship all your belongings?"

"I'm not taking anything with me. Just clothes."

My mouth dropped open a little. I couldn't speak.

"Jamie, there's no room for all my stuff. Your mom says the condo's fully furnished so I won't have to worry about it."

"But you love your—"

"They're just material things. Nothing I can't live without."

I heard the catch in her voice and stopped myself from pushing the issue. The last thing I wanted to do was make my dear, sweet grandmother cry—or make me cry in front of her. Inside, I knew how important her things were to her even though she brushed them off as insignificant possessions. I made a mental note to call Mom when I got home and find out if there was a way for her to take some of them. At least, her bed. She loved her sleigh bed, and it was the very reason I'd bought one too.

Grandma cleared her throat and topped off our coffee cups. "So, let's talk about something else. How's that apartment of yours? Did you get all settled in?"

I forced a smile and shoved the matter of moving to Florida to the back of my mind. "Yeah, I'm unpacked now and it feels nice to have all that turmoil behind me. I put that quilt you made me on my bed. And the pillow cases you cross-stitched. I love them so much."

Grandma's shaky hand came across the table and squeezed mine. The coolness of her touch warmed my heart. Ever since I could remember, she had poor circulation and cold limbs. It was what made her different from my mother, whose hands were warm and strong.

Grandma, despite her limitations, seemed to know me better than anyone. She saw right through my idle chit chat and said, "I love you so much too, Jamie."

Chapter Eight

After coffee, Grandma and I moved into the living room to do a little crocheting. She showed me a new stitch she'd been working on and I, of course, stuck to my beginner's chain. For hours, we talked and looped, and I, being distracted by my depressing thoughts, took a few moments here and there to text Joseph. Without him realizing, his little messages helped me get through the afternoon, especially once I found out Candace's Christmas lights had been successfully taken down without injury. Part of me wished I was there helping him pick out his sister's Christmas tree. But no sooner than I wondered about his progress, he texted me two pictures and asked me to choose the one I thought Candace would prefer. Even though we were apart, I felt I was there with him.

At four thirty, my grandmother looked up from her crocheting at the chiming grandfather clock and tucked her yarn and needle in the basket at her feet. "I should freshen up before Joseph comes."

She labored to get out of her recliner, and I dropped everything to assist her. It didn't go without its reprimand as she insisted she didn't need help. I allowed her to stand on her own, but kept my hands inches from her body in case she fell backward.

She shuffled toward the bathroom. "I'll just be a minute."

I cleaned up our empty coffee cups and cookie crumbs and did the dishes for her. Afterward, I ambled around the house, looking at old pictures hanging on the walls. Each photo led me closer to her bedroom and I eventually made my way inside.

If Grandma was anything, she was a clean freak. Her bed was made, her dresser tidy, and not a speck of dust could be seen on the furniture. I wondered how long it took her each day to dust and clean her house given every movement she made was slow and painful.

I sat on the edge of the bed and ran my hand across the quilted fabric of her comforter. So much love and care had gone into those stitches, and it made me sad to think she'd leave it all behind—just to keep from being a nuisance to her loved ones.

My heart ached as I thought of all the things my dear grandmother was about to sacrifice. As a woman who lived through the Depression, watched her husband go off to war, and worked for minimum wage to help make ends meet, she'd given up so much already. It hardly seemed fair she should be made to do without in yet another chapter of her life.

I placed my face in my hands and cried. I cried as silently as I could so Grandma in the bathroom wouldn't hear me. A gentle knock sounded and I jerked my head upright. Joseph stood at the bedroom door, his face full of concern.

"You all right?"

I sniffed and wiped away my tears, feigning a smile as I scooted off the bed. "Yeah, I'm fine. I didn't hear you pull up."

He thumbed behind him. "Your grandmother let me in. She said you might be in here." Joseph approached me and placed his hands on my shoulders. "What's wrong?"

"Nothing," I lied, trying to shrug off his grasp.

He halted me and tugged me back into his arms. "Don't lie to me, Sutherland. You suck at it." His eyes bored into my soul. "Seriously, what's wrong?"

I tried to keep my emotions in check. I glanced out the doorway, checking to make sure Grandma wasn't within earshot. His hand cupped my cheek and directed my eyes toward his.

"What is it?"

I laid my hand over his and felt the comfort of his large knuckles press into my palm. My eyes burned as I struggled to get the words out. "Grandma just told me some news after you left that's hard to swallow right now."

"Is she all right? Is it her health?"

"No, nothing like that." My voice didn't sound convincing. I felt the hard lump in my throat swelling. "She's selling the house and moving to Florida with my parents."

His eyes widened. "What? Why? She loves this house. What would make her decide to do that?"

Joseph's rapid fire of questions made me smile a little. At least I could say I wasn't so distraught that I couldn't recognize his defense mechanisms. "She told me the cold weather is getting to her and she's decided to take my parent's up on their offer to move where it's warmer. She doesn't want to be a nuisance, she says."

"Nuisance? She's eighty-some years old, for crying out loud. She's earned the right to be a nuisance."

I shushed his rising voice. "No one called her a nuisance outright. She just feels that way because some things are getting more difficult to do on her own. I told her I'd come down here on a regular basis to help her, but she won't hear of it. Her mind's made up, and I have to respect that."

"Okay, so…she's selling and…."

I saw where he was going with this and stopped him. "I already offered to buy the house, but she doesn't want me to. I told her I could afford it, but she's right…I can't commute two hours to work every morning. Traffic would be horrendous, not to mention the two-hour drive back each evening. It's just not feasible." My voice cracked under the weight of this realization. I hadn't wanted to accept it, but in talking aloud about it with Joseph, the conclusion became quite clear. Saving her house was impossible.

His thumb made a delicate swipe across my cheek, catching a falling tear. "Jamie. Don't cry. We'll figure out something."

"There's nothing to figure out. It is what it is, and I just have to come to terms with it." I straightened my back, sniffed away my sadness, and put on a happy face. "I'll get through this."

He feigned a smile just for my sake and pulled me into his embrace. "You have to look at the bright side. At least your grandmother is still here. You haven't lost her forever."

I was glad my face was pressed against his chest. I couldn't bear for him to see me after he delivered those poignant words. Knowing he referred to the pain of a loved one's passing—as only he could attest—it took me a minute to get past pitying him and see his point for what it was.

He was right. I wasn't losing her. She was just moving further south. There were worse things to deal with, and I should be grateful my time with her had not come to an abrupt end.

I squeezed my arms tighter around his body, his thick Carhartt jacket cushioning the vice I had on his ribs. He returned my hug and I could've stayed in his strong, protective embrace all night.

Forcing myself to step back, I lifted my chin to meet his gaze. "Thank you."

"I didn't do anything," he said humbly, his hair falling over his eye.

I clutched his hand and locked my fingers with his. "Yes, you did. More than you know." I gave his arm a little tug, leading him into the hall. He followed without resistance and awarded me with his sweet smile. If we'd been in the privacy of my own home, I might have kissed him senseless. As it was, we were about to take my grandmother to dinner, and as much as I knew she liked Joseph, she wouldn't stand for me to 'get fresh with him' in her home. Her words, not mine.

"Are you two kids ready to go?" I heard her call from the entryway. By the time we turned the corner, I saw her digging into the hallway coat closet. "Joseph, will you be a dear and help me."

He rushed forward, his hand resting protectively on her back. "Sure, what do you need?"

"That thing there, in the back on the left. It's stuck on something." She looked at me accusingly as I walked up beside them. "Probably your Grandpa's work shoes. That man sure had big feet."

"Is this what you need?" Joseph asked, finally freeing a poster-sized metal frame with two legs. As he turned it around, the telltale black and fluorescent orange colors of a FOR SALE sign flashed before me.

My breath caught. Joseph and I exchanged looks, and I could see his was one of sincere empathy. Neither of us could've foreseen this bombshell.

"Yeah, that's it," Grandma said, unaware of my shock. "Your grandfather made that sign when he was selling that old Cadillac he fixed up. Remember that car?"

I shook my head mechanically, still staring at the seven capital letters taunting me as Grandma continued with her story.

"You used to love to lie down in the backseat of that car and stretch out. 'Course, you were only six years old and no bigger than a minute." I heard her laugh as she segued to the story of how I used to be little enough to scrunch down into a beer box and scare the bejesus out of Grandpa's friends.

"Oh, Joseph, you should have seen it. Her Grandpa'd be outside having a beer and when his friends would pull up, he'd say," —and this was when I came out of my trance because Grandma's sweet voice turned deep and loud as she imitated Grandpa— "Get ya a beer there and sit down. They're nice and cold." She laughed, whether at the memory or maybe at the stupidity of his friends who constantly fell for the joke, I didn't know. "And right when they'd reach down to grab a bottle, Jamie here would jump out of the beer box, arms in the air. Like to give ol' Arlin a heart attack that one day, you remember that, Jamie?"

Again, I nodded and faked a laugh over the three-decade old memory. It was good to see Grandma smile, and I realized I needed to buck up. What kind of granddaughter would I be to rain on her parade? Granted, it wasn't a Macy's Thanksgiving Day Parade, but she was happy nonetheless. It was obvious she'd come to terms with selling and I, in my own pessimistic way, needed to as well.

Chapter Nine

We ate dinner at the Grey Goose on Main Street. I tried my best not to dwell on the image of Joseph staking the FOR SALE sign in my Grandma's front lawn before we left. Or how she'd asked Joseph if he would mind fixing her drippy bathroom sink faucet the next time he was in the area. But it was all so overwhelming. Hearing her talk about repairing incidentals so would-be house buyers couldn't whittle her down on the final sale price had me near the breaking point again.

I ate my salad in silence, listening to Joseph accept the job, without pay of course, and how he'd also rid the squeak in her front door while he was there. For the duration of the meal, I hardly partook in their conversations, allowing Grandma to gush and praise Joseph at every turn for being such a gentleman. It wasn't often she let her hair down and enjoyed the company of a young, attractive man, especially one who was going to be practically at her beck and call now that she suckered him into some minor renovations. As a widow, she had every right to cut loose, laugh, and even swoon—if she cared to—over a handsome man's attention. Her innocent flirting and blushing had me valuing her lighthearted spirit that much more. I was definitely going to miss her.

"Jamie, honey, can you help me with my coat?"

Grandma's request brought me back to reality. I looked up and saw Joseph paying the bill as my grandmother flipped her napkin from her lap to the white-clothed table. I jumped up and helped her scoot back her chair, giving her ample room to brace herself and stand. Joseph joined in, sandwiching her between us, in case she staggered.

He and I locked eyes and I mouthed the words *thank you*. I meant for both dinner and for being so attentive to Grandma's needs, though I think he assumed the tab. He smiled, until she yanked on his arm and wound her own around his elbow. His laughter tickled my insides as he accepted his role of being her escort for the evening.

"Don't forget your coat and scarf, Grandma," I reminded her, wrapping them around her snuggly. She barely surrendered her death grip on Joseph as she sifted her arms through the sleeves.

Patting his hand with hers, she smiled up at him. "You're a nice young man, Joseph. Should I leave the tip?"

He picked up her purse from the chair and swung it up on his shoulder. "Your money's no good here, Rose. I took care of it already."

She harrumphed and walked arm-in-arm past the other patrons in the restaurant. I trailed behind them, unable to see Grandma's face but I imagined she was eating up all the envious glances from the other mature ladies in the place. Joseph was naturally a sight for sore eyes in any room. Coupled with his dashing smile and attentiveness to the elderly, tonight he was twice as fetching.

Walking out into the street, Joseph continued to speak to my grandmother with his arm still buried between hers and her bosom while she cooed over every charming thing he said. If she'd been anyone else on his arm, I might have been jealous.

As the three of us walked a few car lengths down the sidewalk to Joseph's truck, my eyes happened to drift downward. His sexy, tight little Wrangler butt was all mine to ogle. I took advantage of the moment—I certainly needed the distraction—and studied how his jeans hugged him with just the right amount of give in the fabric to accommodate the alluring bulge of his ever so sculpted, taut behind. Mesmerized by his perfect physique, the zigzag stitching on the back of his pockets lulled me into a lazy stupor. My brain drifted to thoughts of me slipping my hands into both said pockets and cupping that perfect butt like nobody's business. And then I'd—

"Jamie!"

The sharp snap of Grandma's voice cause my head to jolt upright. Joseph was peering over his shoulder at me, his brow cocked. "Whatcha doin' back there?"

"What?" All coherent brain function scattered.

"Do you need to borrow my hearing aids, honey?" Grandma joked. "I said, take my purse so Joseph can hoist me in this truck."

"Right." I circled around them and hefted her purse onto my shoulder, the weight of it surprising me. "What the heck you got in here, Grandma? The kitchen sink?"

"Just a lady's necessities, dear."

All ten pounds of it, I imagined. *Criminiddly, it was heavy.*

I watched as Joseph stood directly in front of Grandma, his hands on either side of her waist, and gently lifted her body enough so she could place her foot on the running board. Straightening her leg, she slid herself onto the seat of his single cab truck.

She let out a 'whoo' and a sigh to follow, patting Joseph's hand. "Thank you, good man."

"My pleasure, ma'am."

"Rose," she corrected with a smile.

I placed her purse on her lap and told her I'd buckle her in from the other side. Closing the door, I met Joseph's eyes. His grin foretold of a devious thought, one that looked especially sinful under the dim white glow of the street lights.

He wrapped his arm around me as we made our way around the front of the truck. "Did you enjoy the view?"

"What?"

"The view. My ass."

"I was not looking at your ass."

"Right."

"I was just daydreaming, Joseph."

His laughter carried in the night as he opened the driver's side door for me. "I believe you."

I stepped up onto the running board and smiled back at him. It was all I could do after being caught red handed.

"Might I partake in the same shameless goggling? It's only fair," he added and gave my rump a firm slap.

I jumped at the playful spanking, quickly plopped myself on the front seat, and slid over to the middle. I pointed at him and flashed him a look that said 'Behave. My grandmother's watching.'

He climbed into his seat and winked. He inserted the key and the engine roared to life at the same moment he complimented my derriere.

"What did he say?" Grandma asked, handing me her seatbelt buckle.

"Joseph was just remarking about how good the food was tonight." Where I came from, white lies were not sins, especially when they were said to protect my grandmother's delicate sensibilities. After hearing the click of her seatbelt, I turned to retrieve mine.

"It was *so* good," he boasted, grinning like a sly fox. "Wishing we had leftovers."

I elbowed him as a warning before Grandma caught on. "Just drive."

He chuckled, peeking into his side-view mirror, and pulled away from the curb. His leg rested against mine as he shifted smoothly through the gears, and the warmth of his body heated places in me that were far too scandalous to mention with my grandmother sitting beside me.

In a matter of minutes, Joseph turned the corner onto her street and that darned FOR SALE sign caught me off guard again. I stiffened at the blow and clenched my jaw. I'd forgotten about it for a few blessed minutes given Joseph's grand scheme of distracting me. But there it stood, like an ostentatious nudist on a non-nudist beach, flaunting its bold message in all caps.

Joseph must have felt my reaction. He switched hands on the steering wheel and laid one on my knee, giving it a reassuring squeeze. Pulling into the drive, I closed my eyes. I could barely look at my grandmother's house knowing this might be the last time I'd be allowed in it. I didn't think the new buyer would be all that willing to let me frequent the rooms I loved as a kid.

Grandma reached down and unbuckled her belt, slapping her heavy purse in my lap. "Well, Jamie, it was so nice of you to come by today."

I wanted to say we'd do it again, as that was my normal response, but I clamped my mouth shut. Instead, I just faked a cheery smile.

Joseph had already exited the truck and made his way to the passenger-side door. When he opened it, brisk night air sifted inside and stole the little warmth left in the cab. I watched as Grandma rotated in her seat to allow Joseph to help her descend. With the debonair of a true gentleman, he set her on her feet and guided her up the driveway to her porch steps.

I scurried from the truck to meet them, digging in her purse for the keys. I unlocked the door and held it open so Joseph could walk her inside. I enjoyed how he took the time to help her out of her coat and hang it in the hall closet. No other boyfriend of mine had ever been so attentive to my grandmother, especially without prompting. I suppose it was all natural to him growing up in a predominantly female household where good manners were important. I made a mental note to thank him for his courtesy on the drive home. Maybe even give him "a little sugar" for his trouble, as my grandmother would say.

"Now you make sure you lock up behind us, Grandma." I set her purse on the entryway table and gave her the tightest hug her osteoporotic bones could handle without them crumbling to dust in my arms. "I love you so much."

"Oh, Jamie, you know I love you too. And don't you fret about me moving to Florida, you hear? Everything's going to be just fine."

"I'll try."

Sounding convinced was not my forte when I had to sell something I didn't believe. How would everything be just fine when I was not only losing the house I'd adored for as long as I could remember, but my precious grandmother as well? I teared up thinking about the hundreds of miles that would soon separate us.

"Now, don't you start that," she remarked, shaking my arm. "We still have Christmas to celebrate together. We can cry then."

I laughed a little and stepped toward the door. As Joseph said his goodbye, her eyes twinkled like I'd never seen before. Not only was Joseph good for me, but it seemed he was twice as therapeutic for her. I'd remember this night and how happy she'd been in our company for the rest of my life.

Chapter Ten

"You're awful quiet, Sutherland. You okay?"

Joseph's tender voice broke through the haze of my depressing, woe-is-me thoughts. I couldn't even tear my gaze away from the starry night outside my window for fear I'd break down. I took a deep breath and blew it all out before choosing my words.

"Yeah, I'm fine. Just wish there was some way to save Grandma's house. She's not even taking her stuff with her," I added in frustration. "How can she walk away from all her precious possessions?"

"Maybe they're not as precious to her as you think. Maybe they're reminders of who she used to be. A wife. A mother. A grandmother to you. Taking them with her might only hark back to a place and time she'd rather be. Sometimes parting from everything you've ever known is easier than bringing it all with you. Clean slate, you know?"

Joseph's words did little to soothe my aching heart. In time, I'd probably look back on his wise words and realize just how sensible they were. Right now, I was content to sulk.

"Hey," he said, stretching his arm toward me. "Come here. Slide over."

Reluctantly, I unbuckled and skimmed across the seat toward him. After securing the other seatbelt, his strong arm tugged me closer until my body nestled right against his. I leaned my head on the pocket of his shoulder and relished the security I felt in his embrace. Just nestled up to him made a world of difference to my mood.

"Thanks for all you did this weekend," I finally said. "You have no idea how much it all means to me."

"I've got a pretty good idea."

I heard the smile in his voice without looking up. Joseph's handsome smiling face had been the one thing that struck me on the day we first met and it would forever be the warm sunshine on all my cloudy days. "I know I didn't say much about our date last night, but I hope you know how happy you made me. No one's ever done anything remotely close to that. The lights, the dinner, the dancing...I'll never forget it, Joseph."

"Neither will I. Speaking of," he said, reaching into his coat. "I believe this is yours."

I watched him pull out a CD case from his breast pocket and hand it to me. I smiled as I held my Frank Sinatra greatest hits—the one he stole from my apartment. "Oh yeah, I almost forgot about it." I had to laugh as I remembered how he'd waltzed into my bedroom uninvited and begged me to just get in the truck with him. To trust him enough that he'd make everything all better. Little did he know I'd trust him enough to walk through broken glass, if he needed me to.

"Why don't you put it in, DJ? We could use a little pick-me-up right now."

I plucked the CD from its housing and slipped it in. Ol' Blue Eyes started singing one of my favorite tunes and I snuggled back into my spot under Joseph's arm. Nothing else was said as we made our way up I-75 North and that was fine with me. I think after all that had happened to us in the past twenty-four hours, we both welcomed the peace and quiet.

As we finally crossed the Brent Spence Bridge, the downtown lights of Cincinnati, combined with the nostalgic Sinatra melodies playing in the background, welcomed me home. As much as I loved visiting with my grandmother, the sight of familiar landmarks brought an unspoken sense of comfort to me. The PCN Tower, the Great American Tower with its top inspired by Princess Diana's tiara, the Carew Tower, and so many other architectural wonders of the Queen City lit up the night. They stood proud and tall as if saluting my safe return.

Weaving through Cinci's streets, Joseph gave my body a little squeeze. "You asleep? We're almost home."

Hearing him say that made it sound like we shared a home—which we did in a sense since we lived in the same apartment complex. But my brain took it further. I liked the sound of living with Joseph, though I'd never mention such a thing to him. Previous relationship faux pas warned me of that mistake, and I'd be darned if I was going to give Joseph a reason to back out now.

"No, I'm not asleep. But I'm ready to."

He parked the truck in the side lot and killed the engine. Without hesitation, he leapt from his seat and held out his arms for me. I retrieved my purse from the floorboards and slid across, taking his hand. I heard the hard slam of the door and the beep-beep of the lock mechanism engage before he wrapped his arm around my shoulder. We walked together into the building and stepped onto the elevator.

I looked up at Joseph after he pressed the button for our floor and the doors closed. For a few seconds, we were shut away from the rest of the world, except for maybe the guy on the other end of the hidden camera. He turned his head and smiled down at me. "What?"

"Caroline is so wrong about you," I said. "You've got the biggest heart of any man I've ever known."

His deep chuckle echoed around me. "Glad you think so. And while we're on the subject of Caroline...I'll be changing my locks this week. We don't need another surprise visit from her."

I was relieved he'd go to such lengths to keep Caroline from entering his life again. It proved to be a very bold act of finality on his part. And I was ever so happy for it. "You think that'll keep her from trying?"

The elevator doors opened and we stepped out, still in conversation as we walked down the hallway. "It'll be a start. Maybe she'll finally take the hint."

I baited him before I realized the impact of my words. "And that would be...?"

We stopped at my door and he leaned his shoulder against the wall. That cool casualness of Joseph's demeanor returned as he crossed his arms and gazed upon me with a shrewd grin. "That I've moved on. That I've found someone who makes me happy and accepts me for who I am."

I looked away. Anywhere besides the lure of his handsome face. He was right. I didn't take compliments well. I dug in my purse for my keys.

"Allow me," he said, pulling his large ring of superintendent's keys from his coat pocket. With quick precision, he found and inserted the correct key in the door. He turned the door knob, swung the door open, and gestured for me to enter.

I flipped on my lights and turned around to face him. "Thanks for a wonderful weekend."

"It's not over yet."

I smiled at his attempt to stretch the night a few hours longer. "Well, if it's all right with you, I'd like to be alone for a while." Which really meant turn in early. Eat a whole pint of ice cream. Cry myself to sleep. The usual female eccentricities.

He nodded casually and shoved his thumbs in his pockets. "Sure. Whatever you want."

I began taking off my coat, but he snagged the sleeve and pulled me to him. His long arms trapped me in a comforting hug, his mouth turning up in a scheming smile. "Realize if you decide you need company, or if your room gets drafty, I'm right next door. You could always sleep walk your way over to mine."

My laughter mingled with his, though I imagined he wasn't necessarily joking. "I appreciate the offer, but I'm pretty certain I'll be warm enough in my own bed."

"Can't blame a guy for trying, right?"

"I'll give you points for effort." I relished the way he looked at me with such want. I could never tire of it.

"Are you busy tomorrow?" he asked, taking another swing in the batter's box.

"No, why?"

He crinkled his nose in a frown. "I'm a little behind with my Christmas shopping, and considering how well you chose Candace's tree—which by the way, she loved—I thought maybe you could help me buy gifts for the family."

"You want me to go Christmas shopping with you?" I had to ask because, frankly, I was a bit surprised.

For one, men didn't seem to enjoy that kind of thing. I often recalled my father and brother-in-law grumbling on Christmas Eve about the crowds, the rudeness of so-called *gift-givers* ripping sale items right from a person's grasp, and the fact that it was ultimately a waste of time given their wives would return whatever they picked out anyway.

Secondly, Christmas shopping as a couple projected all the signs of a committed relationship. Surprise, surprise. My pessimism crept forward. I couldn't help it.

"Yes, I do," he reassured. "I could use your help—if that sounds like something you wouldn't mind doing on a Sunday afternoon."

I'd give this man a lifetime of Sundays. "I'd love to. What time you thinking?"

"Noonish?" he pitched. "We'll grab some lunch first and maybe head up to Kenwood?"

"Sounds good to me."

"Great." His gleaming smile met his Montana-blue eyes. Mesmerized by the intensity of his gaze, I watched with eager anticipation as his mouth neared mine. He stopped just short of my lips, his arms hugging me tighter against his chest. "Sleep well, Sutherland."

Our mouths touched and my knees buckled. Ice cream and a good cry no longer held their appeal. Josephs' kiss was much better for the soul. Beyond compare. No denying, the man knew exactly what he was doing when it came to physical touch. His hands, his lips, the way his body moved forward and connected with mine in all the right places. Every part of him worked together in perfect harmony to deliver the best kiss imaginable.

He smiled as he pulled away and stepped out of my embrace. He backed up into the hall, clenching his jaw as he held my gaze. The look on his face displayed the pain he endured at parting from me. I wondered myself how long I could keep up this charade of celibacy. It had been a long time since I'd wanted a man this badly. Heck, it had been a long time since I'd had any kind of desire—period. And Joseph, with all his chivalrous qualities and drop-dead gorgeousness, only made it twice as hard to resist that temptation.

"Goodnight, Jamie."

I sighed and nodded in disappointment. It was best that I let him leave, though my entire body screamed otherwise. I stepped forward and clung to the door, forcing myself to close it. "Goodnight, Joseph. I'll see you tomorrow."

I heard a small, manly groan escape him, though I know it wasn't meant for my ears. Until I heard his door open and close, I held mine open just a crack in case he changed his mind.

I waited to the count of five. No such luck.

Chapter Eleven

I tossed and turned the entire night. Between thoughts of Joseph sleeping in nothing but his skin-tight boxer briefs and my grandmother moving, I barely got any sleep. The next morning I lugged my tired self from bed at six o'clock and stalked to the shower. A cold one would do me good for multiple reasons.

Afterward, I made a pot of coffee, cleaned the apartment, and caught up on my laundry knowing I'd be gone all afternoon shopping with Joseph. At ten o'clock, I resorted to calling my mother about Grandma. I plopped down in the dining room chair and waited for her to answer. I stared out my windows. Funny how the gray sky hovering above the Ohio River mirrored my mood. I brought my legs up to my chest and hugged them tight as I sipped my third cup of coffee.

"Hey, Mom," I said drearily.

"Well, hello, Jamett."

I cringed every time she called me by my birth name. "How's Dad?" I said out of habit.

"Oh, he's fine. He's practicing his golf swing in the living room again. The man acts like he's going to play Tiger Woods one day." I heard her cover the phone before yelling to him about her precious lamps. "I'm serious, Roger! You break one thing and I'm going to break that club over your head."

I heard Dad reassure her and my mother moan in response. "I'll be glad when we move to Destin and he can practice his swing—on an actual golf course!" she shouted, loud enough that Dad could hear.

"Yeah, about that, Mom. Is it true that Grandma is selling her house and moving to Florida?"

"She said you paid her a visit yesterday and that you brought a special someone with you. You never told me you were dating anyone. What's his name?"

Leave it to my mother to redirect the conversation to other subjects. "His name is Joseph Scarbrough and I think he may be around for a while." I tried to alleviate the possibility of a long conversation about my personal life by combining points of interest so we could get back to the original topic.

"Well, that's nice, dear," she said in her very predictable, very complacent voice. "How did the two of you meet?"

I assumed her inquiry was solely for the sake of small talk and not because she cared. "He's my next door neighbor."

"It doesn't sound all that romantic, but I suppose convenience has a way of introducing couples just as well as any other approach."

I realized at that moment where my pessimistic side originated.

"Your grandmother said he's a keeper and a looker. He took you both to dinner and paid, I heard?"

Knowing my mother was probably shocked at Joseph's generosity, I made sure to sell that point. "He comes from a well-off family and knows how to treat a lady with respect."

"It's about time you found someone like that. What does he do for a living?"

Here we go. We've arrived at the part of the conversation where she gets to belittle the man I'm dating and offer her opinions as if I wanted them. I could date a prince of England and she'd still find something to remark about. "He's the building's superintendent."

"A blue collar worker, huh?"

The skepticism in my mother's voice rang loud and clear. I drummed my fingers on the table, anxious to make this interrogation as painless as possible. "He's very handy around the house, a veritable Mr. Fix It." My mind flashed back to the day Joseph unclogged my kitchen sink in his 'shirtless' uniform. I couldn't help but smile. "He's even going to repair some things at Grandma's house." I figured I'd sneak in one last attempt at talking Joseph up before she delivered her final ruling on my incompetence to attract a nice, young man with prospects.

"That's what she says," mother replied, unimpressed. "She also said he's a farm boy. Big truck and everything."

I giggled as I could just hear Grandma raving about Joseph's jacked-up truck and how he had to lift her inside. "His family lives in Lexington. They're into boarding horses so a four-wheel drive vehicle is a necessity on the farm."

"I see. He's sounds quite different from your other boyfriends. Which is a good thing, but I remind you that while his country lifestyle may be appealing, it could be the very thing that separates you. You're not used to farm life with its mud, horses, and manual labor."

I expected this from Mom and waited for her to belabor her point.

"What I'm saying is, be yourself with this guy. I know how you are. You think you have to be the person he wants you to be just so you can keep him interested long enough to fall in love with you, but that's not how it's supposed to happen. You want a man who's interested in the real Jamett Penelope Sutherland."

Ugh, there it was again. That name would be the death of me. "Don't worry, Mom. I'm not starting this relationship off with lies." Recollections of how Joseph came to witness my hypoglycemic episode came to mind. "He knows exactly who I am and what my limitations are."

"Does he know your real name?"

I rolled my eyes. "No, Mother. He doesn't. And what does it matter?"

"It matters because that is you."

"Whether I'm Jamie or Jamett, I'm still me."

"Are you?"

My mother's voice raised so high it sounded like the shrill chirp of a referee's whistle. "I think so."

"Well, all I'm saying, honey, is if you can't be honest with something as simple as your real name, then what about the important stuff like how you cherish your independence. Or how you might very well be the breadwinner given his meager occupation. Some men are put off by that stuff."

"Joseph's not like that," I reassured her as much as myself. "And besides, it's not like we're getting married next month. We just started dating for crying out loud."

"I just want what's best for you, Jamie. Don't let this guy change who you are or make you forget what you've accomplished on your own. A Sutherland woman doesn't need a man. We just enjoy their company should they tag along."

I scoffed aloud. "Is that the line you used to score Dad back in high school, Mom?"

"Hey, he knew exactly what he was getting when he first asked me out. And considering he couldn't stay away means I did something right."

In the background, I heard Dad's rebuttal. "You and I both know that's *not* how it went down, but you keep dreaming, Glenda."

"Don't listen to him, Jamie. He's just bitter because I made him work for that second date. He practically begged for it."

"Begged for it?" I heard him say. "The shit's getting deep now. Where are my waders?"

"Go back to your golfing, Roger. Like your memory, your putting's a little off. Anyway, dear, just take your time with this one and be upfront. In the end, he'll appreciate it."

"Right." I took another sip of coffee in hopes of washing down the dry, cynical advice that was my mother's signature. "So, back to Florida, Mom."

"Oh yeah, we kind of got off-track, didn't we?"

Leave it to my mother to never accept blame for something she'd done. "Is Grandma really going with you?"

"I'm pretty sure that's what she's decided. Believe me, I was as shocked as you, but it only makes sense for her to move with us. Surely, you've noticed her memory slipping from time to time."

"I have," I admitted. "And I know the warmer temps will be better for her arthritis, but I just don't understand why she's not taking any of her belongings."

"Honey, there's really no room for them. Have you seen the amount of stuff she's collected over the years?"

"I know, Mom, but she loves her antiques and yard sale finds. Can't she at least take some of it?"

"Jamie, if I give her an inch, she's going to take a mile. I don't want to be put in a situation where I have to limit her. It's bad enough she has to sell the house."

"Exactly. So, why not let her at least take her bedroom suite with her. You know how much she loves that bed."

"Did she put you up to this?"

I hiked my shoulders up around my ears at Mom's accusing tone.

"I know how manipulative she can be, Jamie. She is my mother, after all."

I sighed loud enough that my mother could hear. "No, she did not. I just hate to see her give up so much of what she cherishes. She may be your mother, but she's not like you. Some things are just plain sentimental to her. Believe me, I'd love to convince you to let her take more, but I know who I'm dealing with. You are *my mother* after all."

I felt a small sense of satisfaction in being able to feed her exact words back to her.

"And don't think I haven't thought of ways to buy Grandma's house so—"

"Jamett Penelope Sutherland, don't you dare. You buy that house and you'll be making the biggest mistake of your life, aside from that one idiot, computer guy you dated who almost stole your identity and took you for everything you had. What was his name? Ficklestein? Mickenschtein?"

"Mom!" I grumbled. "It doesn't matter what his name was." Truth be told, I forgot it anyhow. "Anyway, I'm not going to buy Grandma's house because I know it wouldn't be sensible, but the point is you're family. And you should realize how important some things are to her. I'm not asking you to ship everything she owns to Destin. Just give her a little piece of happiness and let her bring something with her besides her clothes."

"Fine."

I paused, feeling skeptical of my mother's change of heart. "Fine meaning…"

"I'll have her bedroom suite shipped to Destin."

"And her handmade quilt that's on it." Since I had my stubborn mother surrendering, I figured I'd better throw in a few extras.

"Anything else?"

I stretched my legs beneath the table, feeling a foot taller. "Well, if you're asking, how about Grandma's china hutch?"

"Don't push it, Jamett."

I talked to Mom for another half hour about Christmas Eve and how they'd be driving down the day after. I offered to have Christmas Eve at my apartment since all their things would be well on their way south in a moving van. Mom couldn't exactly have company over when there was no furniture to sit on.

She agreed wholeheartedly and I think I heard a little excitement in her voice when I told her she'd get to meet Joseph. After finalizing plans, I hung up feeling better about Grandma's move to Florida. At least for her sake, I was able to extract her bedroom suite from my mother's leave-it-all-behind plans. I may not have been able to buy her house, but I at least sold my point to the queen of pragmatism.

My grandmother would be most pleased.

Chapter Twelve

After I folded the last of the laundry and put it away, I selected a purple sweater, and black leggings for today's attire. Every time I'd been with Joseph, I was wearing a T-shirt and jeans. I decided to get a little dressed up for this occasion and maybe show him another side of me that didn't include a ponytail.

I curled my hair and slapped a little makeup on my face, finishing up with a light layer of lip gloss. I spun one last turn in front of the mirror and smiled at my appearance. Satisfied with my casual, but stylish look, I slipped on a pair of fur-lined, knee-high boots to complete the outfit.

With ten minutes to spare, I grabbed my purse and keys from the entryway table and locked up. I knew I'd be early, but punctuality was always my thing. Joseph seemed like the type of guy who'd admired that in a woman, given the countless times he probably had to wait for Caroline to get ready.

I walked toward Joseph's apartment and knocked. My heart picked up speed as I waited for him to answer. The door swung open and Joseph smiled. My gaze drifted downward over his beautiful, muscled chest and the bright white towel that hung so alluringly on his narrow hips. His hair was wet and my mouth went dry as I noticed a few droplets of water resting on his wide shoulders.

"Hey," he said in his distinctive husky voice. "Don't you look nice."

"Hey," I squeaked back. I cleared the frog in my throat. "And thanks. You look pretty good yourself."

"This old thing?" he joked.

I giggled and blushed at the same time.

"Come on in." He gestured towards his living room. "I'm almost ready."

I sneaked a peak at his lower half as he shut the door behind me. *Ready for what*, I asked myself. *A good shagging?*

I tried not to stare, but he looked so delicious in terrycloth. I could certainly get used to seeing this on a regular basis.

"Make yourself at home," he said, waltzing back into his bedroom.

With Joseph out of my field of vision, I forced myself to take in other things around the room. I noticed his guitar still leaning against the wall same as it had a few weeks ago when I helped his drunk-ass into bed. I wondered if he'd picked the instrument up since then.

"Did you get a chance to talk to your mom about your grandmother?" he called from the other room.

I whirled around, hoping I'd get the privilege of seeing Joseph in his towel again. To my disappointment, he was further into his room and, unless I blatantly entered his 'private chambers', he remained hidden.

"Yeah, I did. And good news! I convinced her to ship Grandma's bedroom suite."

"Did she tell you how soon they're moving?"

"It looks like Christmas Day."

"Wow," he said, poking his head out. "That's just around the corner."

We locked eyes for a few seconds and my heart skipped. He had such a way of looking at me that caused all brain function to come to a screeching halt. He broke our gaze and went back to dressing.

I turned back toward his guitar and reached out to touch the strings. I plucked a couple, thinking how much I longed to hear him play. "Written any songs lately?"

"Nah. Not since a few weeks ago."

I knew the week he spoke of; the night before Caroline ripped his heart out. I felt foolish for bringing it up. "Sorry. I wasn't thinking."

"Don't be," he said, sounding preoccupied.

I looked over my shoulder just in time to see him walk around his room in his boxer briefs. He opened his chest of drawers and pulled out a pair of jeans. I watched mesmerized as his biceps flexed and bulged while he worked to slide each long leg into his pants. He made zipping and buttoning his fly look like a regular strip tease, only in the opposite order.

As he turned to retrieve his T-shirt from a different drawer, our eyes met again. Embarrassed that he caught me staring, I whirled around and pretended I hadn't seen him. I heard him chuckle, but, thank goodness, he didn't call me out on it.

I cleared my throat and walked further into the living room where I wouldn't be tempted to peek into his bedroom again. His couch was black leather, sitting between two oak end tables and their respective lamps. A single photo album, bound in black leather, sat on the coffee table beneath a TV remote.

Curiosity killed me. I wondered what pictures a man like Joseph kept. I cringed thinking he might have a few of Caroline in there. I didn't dare look.

"Okay, I think I'm ready now," he announced as he came into the room. He shoved his wallet into his back pocket and strode right past me to the kitchen. "Want a drink before we leave?"

"No, thanks."

I watched him open the fridge, reach inside for a bottled water, and shut the door behind him. He twisted the cap and chugged the whole thing in one huge gulp. "You sure?" he asked again, holding up the empty container.

"I'm fine."

He smiled and threw the bottle in the trash. "That you are." In a few strides, he came to me and tugged me into his arms. "You okay? You seem a little uncomfortable being in here with me. Are you afraid I'll bite?"

I wasn't befuddled because I was in Joseph's apartment. I was befuddled because I was in his presence after seeing him half-naked. No amount of trying could make my brain forget the smooth skin and strong muscles of his body. Add that to being trapped in his embrace while his amazing cologne made my mouth water and I was definitely a woman who'd been irrefutably knocked off kilter.

"Hello in there..." he said, bumping his nose with mine. "Are we needing food?"

I ran with his suggestion as it was the best excuse. "Yes, I'm starving."

He kissed me quick on the lips and flashed his debonair smile. "Then let's get going before that sugar of yours drops." He tugged me toward the door and lifted his Carhartt from the coat hook. "Where's your coat?"

Forgetting it was mid-December, I sighed. "It's in my apartment."

"You goof. Here, take mine." He handed me a deep brown, bomber jacket. Immediately, the smell of leather and Joseph wafted around me. I slipped my arms inside and pulled the coat over my shoulders. I swam in it.

Joseph laughed at me. "You look cute."

"I look ridiculous."

"Ridiculously cute," he added, zipping me up.

I held out my arms, displaying how the sleeves extended past my fingertips. "I'll just get mine on the way out."

"I'd rather you wear mine."

"Why?"

"I'm hoping when you give it back, it'll smell like you." He leaned in and tucked his nose just under my jaw. I heard him inhale. "I love the way you smell."

Sold! I felt like a fortunate buyer at a highfalutin auction. *Sold to the woman in purple who's a pile of putty in that man's arms!*

"You really like how I smell?"

"I like everything about you," he stated, wrapping his arms around my back. I felt him tug on the ends of my hair as he smiled down at me. "I really like your hair today. I don't think I've ever seen it down."

He strung his hands through my curls and let them cascade around my shoulders. His eyes followed the tresses that hung around me in loose waves and the corner of his mouth inched up. I wondered what he was thinking.

I let him marvel me and I enjoyed every minute of it. To hold this man's attention was like winning the lottery.

I saw his Adam's apple bob as he swallowed hard. His eyes blinked in repetition until they eventually landed on mine. "Shopping," he reminded aloud, stepping back. "We're supposed to be shopping today."

"Yes, we are," I agreed. It was nice to know he was having the same issues I was when it came to being this close.

"Okay," he said, clapping once, as if to preoccupy his hands. "Shopping it is. After you."

We walked down the hall and into the elevator. We stood side by side, gazing up at the numbers lighting up as we descended to the first floor. Before the doors slid open, his hand clutched mine. Swallowed up by his large grasp and oversized coat, I felt so small around him, yet on top of the world. We looked at each other and smiled. These moments when we did nothing in particular would be the things imbedded in my soul.

It was official. I was in love with this man.

Chapter Thirteen

We drove north toward Kenwood Town Centre, heading straight for the Cheesecake Factory. After spending almost two hours eating lunch, laughing, and eating some more—because you can't go to the Cheesecake Factory without ordering cheesecake for desert—we finally arrived at the mall.

The place was packed with people, hoping to score the deal of the season. Crowds never bothered me though. I was used to swarms of eager patrons anxious to get their hands on a sale-priced item. At my coffee shop, we always had a seasonal deal to get people in the door. That was Marketing 101.

While I was there to buy gifts for his family, I could arguably say I was there more for the company. I could do anything with Joseph Scarbrough—watch paint dry, wait for water to boil, count toothpicks—it didn't matter. I'd be the happiest woman in the world, whether we were productive in our gift search or not.

Having to shift around countless shoppers and their bags only made it more necessary for me to cling to his side. With his arm wrapped around me, we browsed through many clothing and shoe stores, Yankee Candle (because I just love the smell), the Apple Store (for his teenage niece—big surprise there), the Disney Store (for his twin nephews), and even the Sunglass Hut just for laughs. We tried on pair after pair, sporting our best poses for every occasion imaginable.

Once we tired of that, or rather the store attendants tired of us, I caught sight of one of those instant photo booths. I tugged him toward it and we crammed inside and pulled the curtain. With our hoard of shopping bags surrounding us, there was no place left for me to sit except on Joseph's lap.

He patted his knee with a devilish grin and I accepted. We put in five dollars, chose sepia for the color and a cheesy heart designed frame that would enclose our four random photos.

"Okay. Serious smiles first," I demanded.

"Fine. Then what?"

"We just make it up as we go."

I felt Joseph's gaze on me and when I turned to look at him, his arms snaked around my waist. "I like spontaneous."

He had slipped his hand beneath my coat and I flinched as I felt his warm fingertips brush against my bare skin. The sensation of his hand running along the small of my back felt far too intimate for such a public place.

I reached behind me and grabbed his hand.

"What? No one can see. My hand's off camera." I could do nothing to stop him and his mischievous grin lit me on fire. While holding my gaze, he hit START.

Snap!

The first picture captured us staring into each other's eyes. I gasped. "Wait, we were supposed to do smiles first."

"Too late now. Smile!" He tickled my ribs and sent me into a fit of giggles.

Snap!

"Joseph!" I said, trying to scold him. But he didn't let up. This time, he buried his nose in my neck and kissed under my jaw. The prickle of his five o'clock shadow tickled me even more. I squirmed and tried to pry him away, to no avail. Our laughter mingled and our bodies mashed. His arms held me tight and my hands clasped his scruffy face as the third picture clicked.

Snap!

"Oh my gosh, Joseph! Stop it! We only have one picture left!"

Joseph glanced at the numbers counting down on the screen in front of us. "Three seconds. Better make it good."

I panicked. "We need a serious one. Hurry!"

"You want serious?" he asked.

But before I could answer, he framed my face with his hands and pulled me to his lips. I froze, feeling the sudden demand of his warm, sweet mouth on mine.

Snap!

I barely paid attention to the final click. I was kissing Joseph Scarbrough in a very confined, very private photo booth and nothing else mattered at this moment. Until I heard a little girl's voice from outside the curtain.

"Mommy, they're kissing."

Joseph laughed against my lips and my heart dropped. "They can see us?" I asked in horror.

"Every bit," he murmured. "There's a screen outside the booth."

I pushed away and scrambled from his lap to see if he was jerking my chain. I tripped on the way out and caught myself just as a mother was yanking her daughter away. Sure enough, anyone who happened to walk by could see everything that went down inside the booth.

"I'm sorry," I called to the bitter parent, but my apology landed on deaf ears.

Joseph climbed out with our bags in hand, his gorgeous smile reaching his blue eyes. "You mean you really didn't know everyone could see us?"

"No, I didn't." I unzipped my coat and fanned my face. "Is it hot in here?"

"It's a little warm, but I don't think it has anything to do with the coat you're wearing."

I slugged his arm. "You're the devil."

He inclined his head and kissed my cheek. "And you love it, Sutherland."

I didn't care to admit it, but I did, and smothering a smile proved futile. "I cannot believe we just did that. You know we pissed off a mother."

"It's not the first time I've ever pissed off a parent. Doubt it'll be the last."

"Well, you better bring your game face at Christmas. You're going to need it with my mom."

"She doesn't scare me," he said, leaning casually against the booth.

"You say that now…"

"And I'll say it the morning after we meet." With a casual glance toward the slot, he winked. "Our pictures are ready."

I sighed and pulled the narrow strips of photo paper from the aperture, anxious to see the evidence of our inappropriate behavior captured on film. I scanned each of the four pictures and had to smile. Each one was better than the last, and I couldn't pick a favorite.

"Let me see." Joseph pushed himself off the booth and hovered over my shoulder. A few seconds of silence followed as we admired the thumbnails. "We look good together."

"You think?" I turned my head to the left and my nose bumped his chin. His lips were right at eye level and I couldn't help but look at them. The smell of Joseph and leather and his warm skin enveloped me as I waited for his answer.

"Nobody looks better with me than you. Nobody."

That statement deserved a kiss. More than a kiss, truthfully, but I was restricted to the amount of reward I could give him in the mall without being arrested for public indecency. I pressed my lips to his and held them there. I inhaled his rich, husky scent. I found myself lingering longer than I'd planned, the sound of footsteps and intermittent conversations from passersby drowning out the thudding of my heart.

I wanted more. So much more. Kissing Joseph felt like splurging on a chocolate volcano sundae and heading straight for the hot drizzle of caramel sauce. Much more of this type of behavior and I couldn't be held responsible for what came next.

I pulled away breathless. "Shopping," I reminded.

Joseph closed his eyes and nodded, blowing out his sexual frustrations in one heavy sigh. "Right. Shopping. Where to now?"

"Spencer's," I said with a smile.

He cocked his brow. "Spencer's? What do we need there?"

A layer of suggestiveness coated his question. "Truth or Dare Jenga."

He narrowed his eyes at me. "Who's that for? Your parents?"

"No, silly. Us."

He grunted once like a caveman and followed on my heels like an eager puppy.

Chapter Fourteen

After a long day of shopping, we dragged our sorry butts to his truck and stuffed his cab full of presents, wrapping paper, boxes, and bows. Before climbing inside, I glanced up at the dark clouds above and thanked our lucky stars the wintery mix of rain and snow the meteorologists predicted hadn't arrived yet. I could only hope the nasty weather held off long enough for us to get all this stuff inside our apartment complex.

On the drive home, we ran through the list of gifts to make sure we hadn't forgotten anyone, while Jason Aldean sang *When She Says Baby* on the radio. I had reached into my purse and pulled out a pen and paper to jot down names for the sake of organization. I tapped my pen to the beat of the song as I checked the list twice.

"I think that's everybody." I looked at Joseph, who was strumming the catchy melody on his steering wheel.

"Everybody but you," he stated.

"Me?"

"Yes, you." He sneaked a curious glance in my direction and shook his head. "You didn't think we were exchanging gifts?"

I stammered. "I—I mean—I—sure, I thought about it but—"

"Let me guess. You once exchanged gifts with one of your past boyfriends and it didn't meet his expectations?"

"Try exceeded." I sighed and slumped into the seat. I hated explaining my past mishaps to him. I would've rather dismissed the whole subject entirely but I could tell from his inquisitiveness that he wasn't about to let this one go.

"See, there was this guy, Michael Dougherty. We'd been dating for about seven months and everything was going great. Close to Christmas, he started making a big deal about the gift he bought me and how excited he was to see the look on my face when I opened it. I, being a woman, assumed it might be a ring."

I glanced at Joseph again. He wore a smug little smile as if he already knew the gift was nothing close to what I'd envisioned. Must be some innate guy code I wasn't familiar with because it never occurred to me that it'd be something else. "I know it sounds foolish, but for the record, things were going great. A ring wasn't so far out of the picture."

"Yeah, you said that already." He turned down the radio so he wouldn't miss a gory detail. "Go on…"

"Anyway," I continued, "I decided to get him something that would equal his gift—assuming it was a ring," I justified, "to show how I really felt about him. So, I bought him an engraved watch. A Roger Dubuis. Excalibur."

"Holy crap!"

"I know but, in my defense, I bought it on eBay for only two grand."

"You do realize those babies are worth thirty grand. You sure it wasn't stolen?"

"I don't know. I didn't run the serial numbers."

Joseph was laughing at me now. "This is good. Continue."

Seeing his delight over my predicament made it hard for me not to enjoy my own plight right along with him. I never really laughed over this before, but I had to admit it was kind of comical. Smothering my own smile, I dished out the rest. "So, on Christmas Eve I opened his gift first and…"

"And…" he coaxed, anxious for the punch line.

"It was RUSH tickets."

He exploded with laughter, a hearty bout of guffaws that echoed in the limited space of the truck cab. "He gave you concert tickets?"

"Yes. And I hate RUSH."

He pounded out his delight on the steering wheel. "This is just classic, Sutherland! Concert tickets. How funny is that?" He finally caught my glare and realized his reaction might have been a little over-the-top. He cleared his throat and wiped a tear from his eye. "Sorry. I shouldn't have laughed so hard, but surely, by now, you have to see the hilarity in it?"

"Ha, ha. Yeah, it's so hilarious," I mocked.

With a huge smile, Joseph reached over and took hold of my hand. "I didn't mean to poke fun at you."

"Could've fooled me."

"No, seriously, I get it. Exchanging gifts can be awkward."

"Yes, thank you," I said, relieved to know he understood the point I tried to make. "Especially since we've only known each other a few weeks."

"Okay, so how about this?" he prompted, squeezing my hand gently. "We don't spend any money on each other. The gifts we exchange should be something we already own."

I'm sure I looked thoroughly confused. "You do realize I'm a woman, Joseph. I don't have anything in my possession that a man would want or need—and just so you know, Michael Dougherty kept the watch. If you're looking to score an Excalibur, it's not gonna happen."

"I don't want a watch," he reassured. "And besides, I'm a man. I don't have feminine things in my possession either. But I know we're both creative. We can figure this out."

"I don't know." I grimaced at the thought of making a Christmas gift for Joseph. The first thing that came to mind was a dreaded mixed tape. And yes, I've been there and done that before, with disastrous results. "I think setting a price limit would be easier."

He lifted my hand and kissed my knuckles. "Christmas is about giving from the heart. I'm sure you can come up with something without digging into your wallet."

"You have a lot of confidence in me, Joseph."

"Yes, I do," he agreed. "And I think this will be fun. You and I…exchanging gifts that require a little ingenuity."

Ingenuity sounded like such a typical guy word. Ingenuity, like giddy, was something I did not do.

"So, what do you say?"

"We can't spend a single dollar?" I asked, just hoping he'd reconsider.

"Nope. Not even a penny." He winked at me and held out his hand. "Deal?"

I looked at his hand with reluctance. Finding something I already owned that Joseph would want was going to be a serious challenge. Finding something to give him from the heart would be next to impossible. Thinking I had a little over two weeks to come up with the perfect gift left me with a feeling of utter terror. But if he could do it, so could I.

I think.

I surrendered and shook on it, feeling my world caving in. With a satisfied look on his face, Joseph replaced his right hand on the wheel and drove in silence. By the way he rubbed his whiskered jaw, I knew he was lost in thought, coming up with some ingenious, heartfelt present that would totally put my idea to shame.

My mind was rapidly running through every last thing I owned and evaluating it as a possible gift.

"Did you go?"

"What?"

"Did you go to the RUSH concert?"

I averted my gaze from him and stared out the window at the winter scenery zipping by. "No. He freaked out and took some other chick."

I hoped my answer would be enough for him to drop the darn subject. But no. He had to keep pecking.

"What did the engraving say?"

I whirled my face around, smiling. "Really?"

He couldn't help but chuckle. "Yes. I want to know what you thought appropriate to engrave on his watch."

I scrubbed my hands up and down my face. "Fine. It said *My love for you is timeless.* Happy?"

Joseph stared straight ahead, grinning like I'd never seen him grin before.

* * * *

Just as I expected, sleet bombarded us with icy needles as we unloaded the truck. Somehow we managed to secure all the bags and rush upstairs in one trip, Joseph carrying the most.

I dug his keys from his coat pocket and unlocked his apartment door. We set the packages on the floor and took off our coats.

"You hungry?" Joseph asked as he hung them up.

"Not really. You?"

"I'm a guy. I'm always hungry," He headed toward the kitchen patting me on the butt as he passed me.

I followed him and watched as he took a beer from the refrigerator, screwed off the top, and downed a few gulps. "Wanna beer?"

Crinkling my nose, I shook my head. I hated the taste of beer.

He gazed into his fridge and named the other drinks he had to offer.

"I'm good."

Determined to find something for me, he opened his cabinet. "I've got a little Southern Comfort?"

Feeling a bit chilled from the outside weather, and a little mortified from my dating demise story, a little shot of alcohol seemed the right way to go. "Sure. I'll take that."

Joseph smiled at me, as if he relished the idea of my hidden daring side, and poured me a shot of the amber liquor. He handed the glass to me and clinked his bottle against the side. "To us."

I nodded once and lifted the glass to my lips. I started to sip it, but thought otherwise. I tilted the glass higher and swallowed like a champ. I slammed the glass on the counter and squeezed my eyes shut against the sweet burn in my throat and chest. When I opened them, I saw Joseph staring at me with his bottle resting on his lips.

An easy grin turned up the corner of his mouth. "Get 'er done, Sutherland. Want another?"

"One more," I said without hesitation.

Again, I shot it back and reacted the same way. I clapped my hands once and rubbed my palms together, ready to take on the world. "Truth or Dare Jenga?"

Joseph eventually let out an edgy laugh, still contemplating my unusual mood. "Sure. If that's what you want to do."

I turned to walk into his living room and he snagged my elbow, whirling me around. "Hey. You okay?" He set his beer down and pulled me into his arms. "You're not yourself right now. Is this about exchanging gifts? 'Cause if it is, we can skip it altogether. I don't want you to feel like we have to do this. I'm good with anything. Gifts or no gifts."

I opened my mouth to speak, but clamped it shut. I didn't know how I felt about the whole secret Santa thing. I didn't want to make a big deal over this or make Joseph feel like I wasn't into the idea of a committed relationship—especially if he was. On the same token, I didn't want to make the mistake of assuming how he felt and come up with something that was, like my past blunders, a little too over the top. The last thing I wanted to do was send the guy mixed signals and have him running scared like all the others.

"How about we just play Jenga, and I'll let you know how I feel about it tomorrow."

He nodded, reading me carefully. "We can do that."

"Okay," I said, pushing out of his embrace. His muscled body was getting me all worked up again. "You get something to eat, and I'll set up the blocks."

I didn't wait for him to offer a better suggestion. I turned and dug the game out of one of the shopping bags on the floor. I aligned the stack of red wooden blocks in a tower on his coffee table and sat back on the couch to wait for my handsome opponent to join me.

His photo album stared back at me.

Taunted me.

I moved it to his end table. I hadn't drank enough to open it and see what pictures were inside. I wasn't sure there was enough alcohol in the world for that.

Within a few minutes, he entered the living room with his beer, a plate with a PB&J and chips, and another shot of Southern Comfort. He handed me the glass, set the dish on my end table, and picked up his sandwich. I set my drink aside and watched him shove the last of his sandwich into his mouth as he took a seat beside me.

"Who goes first?" he asked, running his tongue along his teeth. He downed his beer and placed the empty bottle on the floor.

"I will." I assessed the tower and spotted an easy block. With as much stealth as my shaking fingers could manage, I began sliding the little bugger out.

"Any rules I should be aware of?"

I halted immediately, unable to talk and slide at the same time. "It's truth or dare, Joseph. Anything goes."

"Is that the alcohol talking or you, Sutherland?"

I ignored him and finished slipping the block from between its vertical lodging. The tower barely moved and I held my prize with pride.

"Read it," he commanded. "It's not yours 'til you complete the task. You fail to do what it says, it's mine."

"I know how to play the game."

He seized my hand before I could read my block. "Did you play with Michael Dorkerty?"

"Dougherty," I corrected. "And no."

He laughed and shimmied back on the couch. "Just checking."

I stuck my tongue out playfully and read the block. My smile faded.

"What's it say?" Joseph asked eagerly.

"It's a dare."

"Well? Come on...read it."

I drew in a deep breath. "Demonstrate your favorite sexual position."

Chapter Fifteen

Joseph's laughter erupted and he clapped in his excitement. "Perfect. This I gotta see."

I take back what I said before. There was not enough alcohol in the world for me to do *this*. Asking him to reveal the photos in his album suddenly didn't sound like a walk on the wild side.

"Come on, Sutherland. Strike a pose."

I bit my lip. "I think we need a new rule."

Joseph tilted his head to the side. "What's wrong? You having a hard time with this one? It's only the first block. I've never played the game before, but I imagine they don't get easier."

I've never played the game either. I only heard about it from my college days, but no one ever mentioned just how personal the dares could get. I figured they'd be physical challenges or tasks of a comedic nature. Weren't the truths supposed to be of the intimate sort?

"I can't do this one," I exclaimed, flipping the block in his lap. "You win."

Joseph picked up the block and reread it to himself. "Fair enough. This one is pretty personal and given we just started playing, I think we should add a rule. Each player has the ability to forfeit a truth or dare of his or her choosing without getting docked for it." He held the block out to me. When I reached for it, he tightened his grip on it and didn't let go. "Is this the one you're forfeiting?"

"Yes, definitely," I affirmed.

"All right, so what do we do with it?"

I took the block from him. "We add it to the top. Your turn."

I watched as Joseph selected and glided his block free with ease. With an air of haughtiness, which was ever so sexy, he rolled the game piece in his palm until the words appeared. He read it to himself, glancing at me, and then back to the block.

"It's a truth," he confessed. "Describe your worst kiss." He thought for a few minutes and came clean. "I suppose that would have to be with Irene Jacobson."

I was hoping it was with Caroline because that would certainly put my mind at ease if she ever came around again. And I *knew* she would one day. Contagious diseases always had a tendency to reappear once they were in your system.

"It was back when I was a junior in high school. Irene was a little...how do I put this nicely...a little malnourished. And she was the only senior from her class that didn't have a date for the prom."

I listened intently as Joseph continued his story.

"I guess being raised with all sisters, I sympathized with the whole female thing about how important it is to have a date for the senior prom. I hadn't asked anyone yet, and I figured I'd make her dreams come true. So, I asked her and she accepted. I think she might have even peed her pants a little that day. Or so the rumors had said. Fast-forward to the evening, I met her folks and she came staggering down the stairs in her frilly, puffy, lacey dress. I didn't think much of it because she wasn't exactly the most graceful girl in school and chalked her unsteadiness up to nerves.

"We arrive at the prom. We dance. She jets off to the bathroom. We talk. She disappears again to the bathroom. This happens all night long, but again, I don't think much of it. I'm just a naive teenager. Hours later, I'm standing on her porch saying goodnight, never thinking that all her stumbling or hiccupping throughout the entire night was due to her sneaking shots of vodka from a flask in her purse. I thought I'd be a gentleman and end the evening with a nice, peck on the cheek."

I could already tell this story was about to head south real quick. A smirk started to inch up on my lips before I could stop it.

"I bent to kiss her and she lunged forward, locking her lips with mine. At first I was stunned, but then as the kiss wore on, it wasn't so bad. Until…"

"Oh no," I murmured, my face puckering at the thought of what the lush did next.

"Yep. She threw up in my mouth."

I didn't mean to laugh, but it was so disgusting I couldn't stop myself. "What did you do?"

"What do you think?" Joseph said, laughing right with me. "I ran off the porch and vomited too. Her father came outside, hearing all the commotion and after he saw the two of us puking our guts out, he accused me of getting his little girl drunk so I could take advantage of her. As if…" he waved.

"What did you say to her father?"

"I took one look at that poor girl, knowing the humiliation she felt was enough to kill her, not counting that she'd have to confess to confiscating a bottle from her parent's stash on prom night. So I went ahead and took the blame."

My laughter died slowly and I looked at Joseph with budding admiration. "That was really sweet of you."

"Whatever. It sure taught me a lesson, if nothing else."

"Oh, yeah? What's that?"

"Never listen to my sisters." He jumped up from the couch and headed toward the fridge for another beer, probably to wash the seventeen year-old memory of vomit from his mouth. Upon returning, he chugged a couple swallows and plopped his block on the top. "Your turn, Sutherland."

I turned my attention to the tower and plucked one from the bottom middle, hoping this one would be an easy play. I read it and my head fell back on my shoulders. "You've got to be kidding."

Joseph held his beer bottle to his lips. "What's your doom now?"

"Blow a raspberry on someone's tummy."

He set his beer down on the coffee table and yanked up his shirt, revealing a luscious rippled plane of rock-hard abs. "Pucker up, Buttercup."

Maybe it was the two shots of courage I'd downed moments ago, but for some reason I wasn't nervous about planting my lips on Joseph's flat stomach and blowing to my heart's content. In fact, I don't think wild horses could've stopped me.

I leaned over, bracing my hands on his thighs—my, my, they were warm from beneath his jeans—and I pressed my lips just above his cute little navel. I giggled at first, failing to make a good connection.

"Do over," he said, his muscles tensing. "Come on, Sutherland. You can do it."

Drawing from his encouragement, I tried again, this time crushing my mouth to his smooth, warm skin. I took in a deep breath and blew for all I was worth. The silly sound we both longed to hear erupted like someone passing gas, and we laughed until we cried.

He high-fived me, and I sat back on his couch. Between the alcohol, embarrassment, and hysterical laughter, I felt hot and triumphant at the same time. I fanned my shirt to stir some much needed air against my clammy skin.

Joseph rubbed his jaw, looking at me oddly. "My turn."

I gestured toward the tower. "Good luck, Giggles."

"Nah," he said, slanting toward me. "I don't mean it's my turn to play. I mean it's my turn to blow a raspberry."

I looked at him, hoping he was only joking. But the second he leaned toward me, I scooted further along the length of the couch. He followed my movements until I hit the armrest and had nowhere to go. Joseph braced his arms on either side of my body, trapping me in a semi-reclining position. I pushed on his shoulders as he threatened to lower his mouth to my stomach. "Joseph, that's not how you play. You can't steal an opponent's dare."

"Who says I can't?"

"It's in the rules," I bartered emphatically.

"I let *you* make up a rule on the fly. So here's *mine.*"

His arms flexed and he lowered himself along my lap. "Joseph...." I tried to sound stern, but the rest of the words failed me. I stared at him as he nudged my sweater up with his nose. Chills ransacked my body, followed by another wave of heat, as I contended with the erotic image of his handsome face at my navel.

I felt like a scared cat, ready to spring at a moment's notice. I lay tense and trembling, my eyes glued to him as he gazed at my bare stomach. A sea of dazzling blue flashed before me as he looked up from his sprawled position. His sexy, devious smile replaced his boy-next-door grin, and I knew I was in serious trouble.

I tried to speak one last warning, but his name came out in the most strangled fashion. Barely a whisper. He held my gaze as his mouth pressed ever so tenderly upon my flesh. The scruff of his beard prickled me, while his warm, steady breath caressed my skin.

I felt him draw air. It was so slow and so deep that I wondered if he was inflating his lungs or relishing the scent of my skin. Without warning, he sank into the softness of my tummy. Ridiculously ticklish vibrations assaulted me as he blew. I squirmed, and yelled, and giggled, and squirmed some more, trying for all I was worth to push him off me.

"Joseph, Joseph, please! I can't take it any—" My useless pleading was cut short by my silent, stomach cramping, heaves of laughter. We writhed and thrashed upon his couch until he finally withdrew his face.

I lay panting in a heap of exhaustion, my eyes closed. When I opened them, I found Joseph looking at me, his face inches from mine. His hair was a tousled, darling mess. His chiseled face was edgy and serious. His eyes grew dark as our breathing settled one ragged breath at a time. I fell entranced by his silent stare. The look of unadulterated desire in his eyes mixed with the lingering scent of cologne and Joseph played havoc with my senses.

I swallowed. Hard. I brought my hands up and cupped his face, unable to look away from the beautiful sight that lay upon me. I could feel myself shaking and I didn't know if I had the guts to initiate what my body craved to do with this man.

I closed my eyes and went in blindly. Our lips met and every muscle in my body relaxed. My heart melted as I felt the heat of his kiss. Passion ran amuck the minute his tongue touched mine and together our bodies entangled like balled-up yarn. On their own volition, my legs wrapped around his back and I pulled myself closer to him. The weight of his body pressed me further into the leather cushions. I was tingling all over and only Joseph could remedy my yearning.

Suddenly, he pulled away, winded and red-faced. His eyes bore into mine as he seemed to struggle with something. I could almost hear his thoughts churning. Should he continue? Should he stop? Should he get up and slam his erection in a door?

"Joseph," I whispered, wanting to alleviate the ethical questions running through his mind. "I think we need a new rule."

He cleared his throat, taken aback. "Another one?"

"Yes." I played with the soft hair on his nape as I tried to find the right words. "I think you and I should stop fighting the inevitable."

"The inevitable being?"

Dang him. Was he really going to make me spell it out? "Being that I want you to—"

He pressed his finger to my lips and silenced me. "Don't say it," he commanded huskily.

"Why?"

I saw his throat bob as he swallowed. "Because I don't want to." He squeezed his eyes shut and recanted. "I mean, I want to. Like, *really* want to. But I can't do that to you."

"Do what?"

He sighed. "Take advantage of you."

"But you're not. I want this." *I think*. Well, ninety-five percent of me wanted this. The other five percent was my wary heart. Majority rules, right? "I'm giving you full consent, Joseph."

His face softened and he smiled. He stroked my cheek ever so tenderly with the back of his hand as he looked at my entire face. My eyes, my lips, my nose, my eyes again. "And you have no idea how much that means to me," he whispered. "But you've had a couple shots. Your inhibitions are gone. I refuse to take advantage of that fact."

My heart plummeted, though I believe with relief rather than disenchantment. The rest of me fell limp beneath him. While I totally gave this man kudos for adhering to the gentleman's code, I was still left disappointed. Combine that with my pessimistic mind and I couldn't help but think perhaps he didn't want me like I wanted him.

"Jamie, please don't think I don't want you. You have no idea how hard this is for me to turn down your offer. It's killing me. I want you more than I've ever wanted anyone." He emphasized his point by crushing his lips to mine and breathing me in. "But," he exhaled, "the last thing I want is for you to wake up tomorrow morning and regret what we've done. I don't want you to have one single doubt in your mind. And I know you. You have doubts that number like the stars."

A guilt-ridden smile eased upon my lips. He was right. I probably would second guess the night and what had happened. I'd relive it over and over in my head, wondering if I'd made the right call. Wondering if those two little shots of courage had anything to do with it. Wondering if Joseph accepted because he knew I was under the influence and this might be his only chance.

Yeah, he was right. It seemed he knew me better than I knew myself. But still the fact remained. I was disappointed and embarrassed and unsure what to even say now. I felt I'd ruined a perfectly good night.

"I'm sorry I came on to you like that," I said, sitting up.

Joseph followed my lead and leaned back into the couch, stretching his legs. He pulled mine across his lap and toyed with the zipper on my knee-high boots. "You don't have to be sorry. I enjoyed it. A little too much, I'm afraid."

I smiled at his admission. "Now what?"

He glanced over at the tower of red blocks. "We could continue to play...."

"Or?"

"Or call it a night. You know we both have to work in the morning."

After all that had happened, I was pretty tired. "I guess we should call it a night."

Joseph fetched my hand and lifted it to his lips, kissing my knuckles. "Not just any night. But one of the best nights of my life." He paused. "You know...I don't think you have any idea how happy you've made me. Being with you has been so different and so...amazing. I've never had this much fun with a woman. With anyone. And I don't ever want it to end. I like believing you and I have something special. Something I've never had before. You're all I can think of. No matter what I'm doing. Your beautiful face is all I see, and it's like sunshine. Warm sunshine." He snapped his fingers. "I think I just wrote a song."

I giggled, letting the warmth of his hand and sweet words caress my soul. As I sat with my legs across his lap, my thoughts were as clear as crystal. I knew I said it before, but some things bear repeating.

I was wholeheartedly, absolutely, without a doubt in love with Joseph Alexander Scarbrough.

Chapter Sixteen

"Jamett Penelope Sutherland, what is that on your face?"

My pen paused mid-sentence as I looked up from the calendar on my work desk. In the doorway of my office stood Melissa, her arms crossed, her foot tapping with impatience. Absently, my hand came up to my cheek. I wondered if I'd missed a dab of strawberry sauce from the Danish pastry I'd eaten this morning.

"Not your face," Melissa corrected, frowning. "Your *face*." She waved her hands in a large circle as if to indicate my aura. "You have the look of someone in love."

I pressed my cold palms against my face to cool my burning cheeks. "Is it that obvious?"

"Honey, Helen Keller could see it." She took a seat on the corner of my desk. "But how is that possible? The last time I saw you, you were near tears over Joseph and his bitch of an ex. Heck, *I* was near tears too." She glared at me sternly. "Don't tell me you went on that date with him after I specifically told you not to?"

I cringed. "I did..." I confessed. "But I had good reason."

"Oh, Jamie..." I could hear the disappointment in her voice. "I knew he'd get to you. You're such a softy."

"Just hear me out, Melissa. Trust me. You're going to love this."

She shook her head. "This better be good."

I pushed next month's scheduling aside and ditched the pen. I sat back in my chair and got comfortable. I knew this would be a long conversation, considering all that had happened since Melissa and I saw each other last Friday night. I sighed. "Gosh, where do I start?"

"Friday night after you left here would be good." The sarcasm in her voice was palpable.

"Okay, so Friday night I went home and got into bed, determined to ignore any of Joseph's attempts to get me to listen to him. And I did," I reassured Melissa. "At least, until he came barging into my bedroom."

"What?"

"Yes, he let himself into my apartment."

"You gave him a key?"

"No, he has a key. To everyone's apartment. He's the superintendent of the building, remember?"

"Oh, my gosh," she said, pinching the bridge of her nose. "I forgot."

"Yeah, well, me too."

"I can't believe he just broke into your apartment like that. I would've called the cops."

"The thought certainly crossed my mind. But I think the shock of him standing in my bedroom in the dark rendered me senseless."

"So anyway...." She churned her hand in a "get on with it" motion.

I reorganized my thoughts and continued. "I sat there in my bed, with the covers pulled up to my ears, and he came to the side of my bed, begging me to talk to him. I told him about Caroline coming out of his apartment early Wednesday morning, and he said he wasn't even in town. He'd been at his sister's in Lexington and had no idea what Caroline was doing there."

"Of course, he's going to say that, Jamie. Men don't just admit they're sleeping with their ex when another chance to score some tail comes their way."

"It wasn't like that at all. He really was in Lexington. His sister confirmed it and she hates Caroline. There's no way she'd lie for Joseph. Besides, wait until you hear why he was in Lexington and what he did for me."

"Well, you better hurry this along. We open in fifteen."

Anxious to fill Melissa in on all the beautiful details of the weekend I had with Joseph, I commenced the long, drawn-out story of our date, how I'd ended up in his bed the next morning, how he'd taken my grandmother and me to dinner, how he'd consoled me over the news of my grandma moving to Florida, how we'd gone Christmas shopping together, and lastly, how we'd played Truth or Dare Jenga. Seeing the look on Melissa's face when I described how I blew a raspberry on his stomach was the best, but seeing her swoon over the fact that he didn't want to take advantage of me once we started making out was priceless.

"I don't know what to say," Melissa uttered as she fanned her face. "What a weekend. What a gentleman." The joy on her face matched the delight on mine as she ruminated over all the glorious details. "I bet you're exhausted. I know I am just listening to you." She clasped my hands in hers. "I'm so happy for you. My little Penelope has finally found true love."

I squeezed her hands and we squealed in unison like immature school girls. Sharing this news with Melissa felt so good. It was twice as gratifying having someone to open up to about the developments in my pitiful dating life, especially when they involved someone like Joseph Scarbrough.

"I could barely fall asleep last night," I conveyed shyly. "My mind kept running through last night, over and over. If only I hadn't had those two drinks."

"I know," Melissa agreed, slugging my arm. "What were you thinking?"

"I don't know. I could just kick myself. But then again, he saved me from the dreaded *morning after*," I said, striking quotes with my fingers. "You know as well as I do that you would've found me in a fetal position under my desk had we done the dirty. Joseph saying no was for the best."

Melissa giggled. "Yeah, you're right. Finding you grinning from ear to ear was much better." She closed her eyes and sighed, relishing my story all over again. "Where can I find a man like Joseph?" Her eyes popped open. "Does he have a brother?"

I slapped her knee as I stood from my chair. "Nope. Sorry."

"Cousin? Distant cousin? Once removed?" she probed, following me out into the coffee shop. "I'm desperate here. I'll take anything."

I unlocked the door and flipped the window sign to OPEN. As I turned to walk back behind the counter, the chimes rang aloud. Melissa's eyes widened momentarily.

"Speak of the devil," she murmured.

I spun and caught sight of Joseph entering with his to-die-for smile plastered on his face. He wore his normal work attire—jeans, boots, and his Carhartt jacket. His chunk of hair was on its best behavior today, but I was hard pressed to forget how messy it had looked last night. Naughty had never looked so good.

I cleared my throat and met him halfway, standing on my tiptoes to kiss him good morning. His arm wound its way around my back as he whispered in my ear. "Good morning, Sutherland." He sneaked a peek in Melissa's direction, noting the huge grin on her face. "I take it she's been briefed."

"I left no detail untold," I said, drawing an imaginary circle on his chest above where his coat gaped. The hard swell of his pec beneath his T-shirt had me itching to tug his cute little self into my office for a little private one-on-one. But I didn't scratch that itch. That would be far too cruel in front of my loyal friend. "So," I finally breathed. "What are you doing here?"

He released his hold on me and eased his way up to the counter. "I just thought I'd grab a cup of coffee before I headed to your grandmother's to fix her stuff."

I walked behind the counter to fill his order. "I thought you were going to do that this coming weekend?"

"Well, I was, but my sister, Randi, called this morning and asked me to help her load some furniture in the U-Haul. Spencer's flying in from Denver to help her pack.

Thought I'd just kill two birds with one stone while I was down there."

"Oh, I see." I didn't mean to sound disappointed, but I was looking forward to going with him to see my grandmother. "I wish I could go with you, but Monday's are Donna's night class at Northern. There's no one to cover for me."

"No problem," he said, leaning over the counter. "As long as you don't mind me hanging out with your grandmother without you."

"No, I don't mind." I thought about how Grandma had gushed over him this past Saturday. "I'm sure she wouldn't mind having you all to herself either. I saw her wandering eyes when you weren't looking."

"Nothing like the way her granddaughter looks at me though."

I caught his charming little wink as I looked over my shoulder and blushed. I couldn't argue with him there and poured some extra frothy cream into his steaming cup of mocha. I didn't bother asking how he wanted his coffee today. I figured I'd give him something to remind him of me for his long drive south.

"You dating anyone, Melissa?" I heard him ask. Without turning around, I knew he'd just piqued her interest with that little question.

"Who's asking?" she replied with a tinge of flirtatiousness.

"A friend of mine. I told him about you and he seemed interested to meet you."

"Is that so?" I saw her eyes light up. "Is he as cute as you?"

"Can't say I ever looked at him that way, but I'd be happy to give him your number, if you're so inclined."

"Oh, I'm inclined," she said in haste. I watched her scratch her number on a slip of paper and hand it to Joseph. "What's his story?"

He tucked her number in his back pocket and smiled. "The usual. Can't find a decent woman to save his ass. Tired of gold diggers and one-night stands."

"Sounds like my kind of man."

I handed Joseph his cup and shook my head at his twenty-dollar bill. "You're doing me a favor by helping my grandmother. Keep it."

He took a sip of coffee and leaned in for a kiss. "I'll see you tonight."

"Okay." I heard Melissa giggle as she turned to help the next customer who walked in the door. "Be careful," I commanded protectively.

"Always." He turned on his heel and almost bumped into the person standing behind him. He apologized and sifted around the long line that had already started to form at the register.

As usual, Melissa and I watched him walk out the door, our eyes glued to his tight Wrangler butt. When the door chimed upon his exit, we both sighed with utter contentment. Having our 'Joseph fix' for the day meant nothing could ruin the start of our manic work week.

Chapter Seventeen

Fourteen grueling hours later, I dragged my dog-tired self from the elevator of my apartment complex and turned the corner of the hallway. Joseph was kneeling at his door, a screwdriver in hand and his trusty Champion toolbox at his side on the floor.

"Hey," I said in surprise. "Watcha doin?"

He glanced up and smiled. "Hey. Just changing my lock. How was your day?"

Mondays always prove to be busy and tiresome. A great thing for an entrepreneur like myself. But hearing Joseph was changing his locks, because of the stunt Caroline pulled last week, totally made my day. No one could erase this self-satisfied smile off my face.

"It was good," I tried to say without much enthusiasm. I didn't want Joseph to know that I was practically dancing a jig on the inside. "How about you?" I slid down the wall beside him. "I didn't expect you to be home so soon."

He looked at me askance. "It is eight-thirty at night."

"Oh, I know," I sighed, closing my eyes. "I just thought you'd still be down at your sister's. How did it go today?"

He made the final adjustments on the new door knob as he spoke. "Great. Your grandma's sink doesn't drip anymore and her door's been squeak-proofed."

"And Randi?"

"The first truck load is on its way to Colorado."

I sat in awe. Joseph was the first guy I ever knew who could be so productive in a single day. Just hearing about how much he'd accomplished had me wondering how the man did it all. Not to mention, drive two hours back to Cincinnati and still beat me home.

He tossed his screwdriver into his toolbox and latched it shut. "You look exhausted, Sutherland."

"I am." He snagged my hand and helped me stand, all the while grinning at me. "What?" I finally asked.

"You haven't said a thing about me changing the lock. You do realize I'm not doing it because it's broken, right?"

I laid my head against his chest, hiding the grin on my lips. "I know why you're doing it."

"And?"

"And I'm thoroughly happy."

He pushed me away from his chest just enough to look in my eyes. "You are?"

"Well, any other woman might run outside, climb the Purple People Bridge and shout it for all the world to hear. But I'm not one to gloat. I'll just celebrate in my own quiet way the day Caroline comes back and finds her key doesn't work anymore."

"Speaking of keys…." He reached into his back pocket. "This would be yours." He took my hand and planted a shiny new key in my palm. "It's only fair since I have a key to your apartment."

I squeezed it tightly. "You sure about this?"

"I've never been so sure in all my life."

He dipped his head and kissed my lips softly. I wrapped my arms around his neck and kissed him back, letting him know just how happy he'd made my evening. When he ended the kiss, I staggered backward.

"Let's get you off to bed," he said, picking up the toolbox from the floor.

"You're going to tuck me in?"

His snicker vibrated through me as he followed me to my door. "If that's what you'd like."

I'd like him to do more than tuck me in, but I wasn't about to confess my most darkest desires to him. I was still a bit mortified about coming on to him last night to traipse down that wicked path again.

I let us into my apartment and turned to flip on the lights. Joseph's hand closed over mine. I heard him set his toolbox on the entryway floor and he kicked the door shut. Holding my hand, he spun me into his arms and kissed me again in the dark. He picked me up in his arms and carried me to the bedroom.

My heart raced. My thoughts whirled. I tensed in his arms and I could feel the sharp edges of his key digging into my palm. I didn't want to let go of it or him. Together, they were such a special gift that I would cherish always.

When we reached my bed, he laid me down. I watched him curiously, wondering what his intentions were. Like a gentleman, he took off my shoes and set them as a pair on the floor. Next, he unzipped my coat and slipped it off me. In seeing my pajamas on the chair, he brought them to me.

He knelt on the floor, between my legs. He reached up and released my ponytail, letting my hair cascade around my shoulders. He played with a curly strand, caressing it between his fingers. "I hope you sleep well, Jamie."

The husky sound of his voice was the best lullaby in the world. Whether he called me by my first name or my surname, I loved the sound of it on his lips. I clutched my pajamas along with his key against my chest. His unruly lock of hair dared me to thread it through my fingers, but I didn't reach out to hold him. I feared I'd not be able to let go.

"Jamie," he said, looking downward.

My voice squeaked. "Yes?"

He looked puzzled or nervous, I couldn't tell. But something consumed him. "Never mind," he recanted, moving to stand.

I snagged his wrist to keep him from leaving. "What is it?"

He brushed back the hair from my face. "I just had a lot of time on my hands today. Thinking, you know. And..." He paused, sitting beside me on the bed. "And I guess I just missed you, that's all."

Amid the dark shadows of the room, I held his hand and gave it a loving squeeze. "I missed you, too. We've spent so much time together lately, it was kind of weird not having you around today."

"Which leads me to my next thought."

"And that is?"

He cupped my hand in both of his. "While I was down at your grandmother's house today, I found a lot of things that needed urgent repair."

"Okay…" I wasn't sure where he was going with this. "So, can you fix them?"

"Sure, I can fix them," he said, tilting his head in thought. "But it's going to take some time. What I mean is, I'm going to be staying with Candace for the next two weeks so I can get them finished on time. You know, before your grandmother moves. I've talked to my boss here and he's fine with that."

"Oh," I said, contemplating this news. "In other words, I won't see you much after tomorrow."

"Right."

"Well, I could always come down on the weekends and help you."

"Actually, I work better alone." My face must have shown my disappointment because he amended his statement pretty quickly. "I'd love to have you there with me, Jamie, but…" His mouth twitched upward in a crooked smile. "I'm afraid you'd only be a distraction for me. I mean, when you're around, I can't seem to focus on anything but you."

His compliment lifted my spirits. A little. "Okay, I get it. I think."

Joseph cradled my face in his hands. "I'll certainly miss you."

I felt bad knowing he was only helping my grandmother because of me. What's worse was knowing he'd not take a cent from her for it and that he was giving up his vacation time to do it. No one was better for the job, but I hated knowing he'd not get anything for his trouble. "I don't expect you to do this, Joseph. I have money. I can hire someone else to do it."

"You're not hiring someone else. I told your grandmother I'd do it for her. I'm not going to back out now."

I could tell there was no convincing him otherwise. "Two weeks, huh?" Saying it aloud sounded more like forever. Being away from Joseph for a few hours was hard enough. Whether he realized it or not, I craved his company.

"Two weeks," he repeated, frowning. "I should get back in town the day before Christmas Eve. Want to get together then?"

"It's a date," I said, already longing for this two-week hiatus to be over.

He wrapped his arm around my shoulder and tugged me against him, kissing my forehead. "In the meantime, you can be thinking about my Christmas gift."

I elbowed his ribs playfully. "What if I've already decided what I'm giving you?"

He laughed. "You so suck at lying, Sutherland." He palmed my face and shoved me. I fell back into the pillows for effect, still clutching my PJs and his key.

"You're so beautiful, Jamie."

"Thank you," I said, reeling inside.

He finally stood and walked to the bedroom door. The longing I felt watching him leave was greater than anything I'd ever felt before. I wanted him to turn around and say how hard it was for him to leave. I wanted him to suggest he stay. I wanted to invite him to spend the night so he'd know what was running through my head.

"Joseph," I called in haste, bolting upright in bed.

He rotated on his heel and braced his arms casually on the doorframe. "Yeah?" His dark silhouette filled most of the opening. He was so gorgeous. What if he turned me down again? I couldn't bear another disappointment.

"Don't forget your toolbox," I said at last.

Despite the shadows masking his features, I could still see the wicked grin on his lips. "Goodnight, Jamie."

Chapter Eighteen

"How long has it been already?" Melissa asked, bumping my hip with hers behind the coffee shop counter.

I cleaned the last of the mess around the espresso machine and tossed the coffee-stained dishcloth into the small sink beside the Styrofoam cups. I sighed and crossed my arms. "Three days."

She gave me a sympathetic smile. "You going to make it?"

"Do I have a choice?"

"I don't see why you just don't go down there this weekend and surprise him. You know you want to."

"I can't. I promised him I wouldn't."

"You don't have to stay all day," Melissa persuaded. "Just for a few minutes. Sneak a little lovin' while he's bent over the table saw."

My brow kicked up. "The table saw? That could get a little dangerous."

She dismissed my literal interpretation with an eye roll. "You know what I mean. Besides, don't you think your grandmother would like to see you?"

"She's not even there," I explained. "Evidently, Joseph is tearing into the walls and there's a lot of dust. He asked my mother if Grandma could stay with them for a while so she's not breathing all that in."

I pushed myself from the back counter and ambled toward the door, my thoughts roaming in the same direction as Melissa's. I wanted more than anything to surprise Joseph with a quick little visit, but I also didn't want to upset him. He made it perfectly clear that I was a distraction, one he didn't need if he was going to get anything done. I turned the lock and flipped the sign in the window to CLOSED.

"What if you surprised him by being at Candace's house?" Melissa suggested. "He's not working there and maybe once he comes home on Friday night, he'll *want* that distraction. He is a man, you know."

As good as that sounded, I was not about to have our 'first time' in his sister's guest bedroom. "I don't think so. I'll just go home and watch some TV. Eat a whole pint of Graeter's."

Melissa laughed at my joke. "Well, if you need anything…someone to help you binge on Black Raspberry Chip or what not, call me. I'll be right over."

"Thanks," I said, hugging her.

"Come on, I'll give you a lift home." We collected our purses and coats and headed out the door together. We walked a couple blocks to the parking garage and climbed inside her cherry red Camaro with black stripes running the length of the hood. I always thought this vehicle had too many horses for her to handle, but they didn't scare Melissa. She lived to test the limits, just short of breaking the rules. I, however, was content to live vicariously through her.

She fired up the engine and pulled out, the deep rumble of the motor echoing against the concrete walls of the near empty garage. In no time, she circled the block and turned down Sycamore Street. She pulled in front of my apartment building and slid the shifter into park. I hugged her from across my seat and got out, waving as she sped away.

Knowing I had nothing to come home to, I entered the historical building in a funky mood. I couldn't believe I had eleven more days of this. I decided then I needed a hobby. Maybe I'd finish that afghan I started crocheting a few years ago. Surprise my grandmother with it for her birthday.

Who was I kidding? Crocheting would only remind me of Grandma, which in turn would remind me of Joseph laboring to repair her house, which then would remind me of how much I missed him. I concluded that I didn't need a hobby after all. I needed more ice cream. Tomorrow, I'd pick up a dozen more pints on my way home from work. Problem solved.

As I stepped off the elevator and turned the corner, I stopped short. Caroline stood just outside Joseph's door, punching an angry text on her cell. I could only assume Joseph was at the receiving end of that stabbing finger. I stepped back and hid behind the corner wall, suppressing a smile. It seemed she wasn't all that happy about the sudden lock change.

Coincidently, my cell vibrated in my pocket. I pulled it out and read the screen.

Caroline is at my door. Don't go home yet.

I texted back.

2 late, already here.

As soon as I hit SEND, I heard the heavy stomps of her designer boots marching down the corridor. I panicked and dashed for the elevator. I pressed both buttons repeatedly. *Come on. Come on.* I glanced up at the floor indicator lights. The elevator was stuck on the first floor. I made a mad dash for the stairwell.

From behind me, I heard the disgust in Caroline's voice. "Uuuugh. You."

I whirled around and manufactured a pleasant smile. "Well, hello. Clementine, right?" I purposely chose a ridiculous name. I was not about to give this woman the satisfaction of thinking she was memorable.

"Caroline," she snipped, planting her hands on her hips.

"Oh, that's right. I'm sorry. I'm terrible with names."

"Cut the crap, Judith." Amazed that the woman was smart enough to dish the name game back at me, I couldn't hide my amusement no matter how hard I tried. My pursed grin only infuriated her. "Do you have something to do with this?" She held up her key between two French-manicured fingernails.

I played dumb. "What's wrong with your key?"

"It doesn't work," she snapped. "Why is that?"

I stuttered, not knowing how to fend off this charging bull. Without a figurative red cape, I felt like an ill-equipped matador. "I don't know. You'd have to ask Joseph about that."

"Oh, I will. Don't you worry. And if I find out you had something to do with this—"

"Are you threatening me?" Somehow, amid all her posturing and hoof scratching, I found my back bone. Standing toe-to-toe with this walking Clinique counter didn't seem to intimidate me anymore.

She glared at me with fire in her eyes. "Where's Joseph?"

As much as it would've pleased me to slap this pompous princess with a full explanation of where he was and why, I wasn't about to divulge such personal information. If he wanted her to know where he was, he would've informed her himself.

"All I know is he's out of town for a couple weeks." I figured I'd give her that much so that in his absence, I wouldn't have to deal with her popping in again.

"Fine," she grumbled, jamming her keys into her purse. She righted the strap on her shoulder just as the elevator door opened and jetted passed me. I watched the doors close behind her as my cell vibrated in my hand.

I smiled when I read Joseph's text.

No matter what she says to make U feel inadequate, remember U have the key that works.

I read his text twice before unlocking my own apartment door, his encouraging words hugging me the way he would—with warmth and compassion. I held my cell as I hung up my coat, wondering what I should text back to him. I reckoned he was worried about our little encounter and was dying to know what went down.

I walked to the kitchen and pulled a half-pint of Graeter's ice cream from the freezer. As the door closed, I caught sight of our photo booth pictures clinging to the front. I plucked the strip from the magnet holding them and gazed at the shots. For the first time since we'd taken them, I regarded each one carefully, recoiling at my goofy poses and facial expressions. But as I studied Joseph's, my heart melted. The camera had captured the blatant admiration in his eyes. If I didn't' know any better, he looked like a man in love.

Staring at the pictures, I snagged a spoon from the drawer and traipsed into the bedroom. Consumed with staring at the two of us as a couple, I absently got ready for bed. My PJs were on, my spoon was primed in the container, and Joseph's apartment key lay reverently on my nightstand. All nestled under the covers, I picked up my cell and texted him at last.

I survived unscathed. Rest assured, what little emotional stress I endured this evening, can be remedied with ice cream therapy.

Within minutes a new text came through.

I'm so sorry U had to deal with this. I will B taking care of it immediately, if not sooner.

Part of me felt sorry for Caroline. Maybe it was the creamy, chocolaty goodness sliding down my throat that eased the burn in my stomach and made me sympathize with her just a little. Giving up Joseph, would have to be the hardest thing she's ever had to do. I'm certain if the roles were reversed, I wouldn't go down without a fight either.

I sucked another heaping mound of ice cream off my spoon and texted a thoughtful reply.

Go easy on her. I'm betting underneath all that scaly skin and fangs lies a heart.

Anxiously awaiting his response, I scraped out the last remaining dollop of ice cream and tossed the spoon into the empty container. Setting the cup on my nightstand, my cell vibrated once more.

This is why I adore U. Leaving UR grandmother's now. Talk to U tomorrow. Gnite

I texted back my farewell, clicked off the light, and snuggled deep beneath my quilt. I laid on my side, gazing at the strip of photos leaning against my lamp and the key propping it up. I hated that I couldn't see the real Joseph or kiss his warm, soft lips goodnight. But I closed my eyes feeling quite content that the man in the sepia photos had strong feelings for me. He may not have admitted his love for me exactly, but his testimony of "I adore you" was good enough.

Chapter Nineteen

In the following days, I kept myself busy working extra shifts. I decided to be a generous employer and give all my college employees some much needed R&R after they came off a grueling, hard-core week of finals. Donna was certainly happy about it, going so far as to bear hug me the day she stopped in to pick up her check.

I even visited my folks a couple nights after work to help them pack and wrap Christmas presents. Grandma, who'd been staying with them while Joseph made the repairs, was extra happy to see me. Of course, when Mom stepped out of the kitchen to yell at my father for golfing in the living room again, she thanked me for convincing my mother to ship her bedroom suite to Florida. Seeing the tears of joy in her eyes was worth every bit of strife my mother had given me. I'd do anything for my grandmother.

Two days before Joseph was due home, I came to the conclusion that it was time for me to quit playing the Good Samaritan for everyone else and grant myself a well-deserved occasion of selfishness. I took a nap right after work, showered, and made a pot of coffee. In the quiet hours of the evening, the recurring thought of Joseph stepping out of his sister's shower clung to my brain. I finally figured out the perfect Christmas gift for Joseph that didn't require the spending of money, like he and I'd agreed upon.

I selected a clean white towel from my bathroom closet and dug into my mess of embroidery thread and needles from a container beneath the bed, choosing a color that matched his Montana blue-sky eyes. Sitting at the table, with the city skyline lighting up the view through the tall windows, I sat down and began stitching. Like my grandmother had taught me, I outlined the letters J, A, and S as a starting point. I monogramed his initials on the towel with the S in the middle much larger than the two beside it. It took me well into the early hours to finish it, but I didn't care. I'd taken the next day off so I could get ready for Christmas Eve at my apartment.

That morning, I enveloped his special towel in matching blue tissue paper and laid it reverently in a long white box. I wrapped the box in blue and silver snowflake paper, topping it off with a large UK blue bow.

Once that was finished, I made another pot of coffee, wrapped the rest of my family's gifts, and began the daunting task of cooking and baking. I wasn't the best chef in the world, but with Grandma's recipes, I could fake it.

Determined to make a dent in the food preparations, I tied on my apron and readied my utensils. I peeled and diced apples for two pies; measured, dumped and mixed all the ingredients for three dozen chocolate chip cookies; and smothered a whole ham in butter, brown sugar, cloves, and beer. I'd made a total mess of the kitchen in just a few hours. Clumps of batter littered the counters, assorted dirty bowls and measuring cups filled the sink, and white, powdery flour dusted every available surface, including my face and clothes. Despite the extra work I'd made for myself pulling cleanup duty, I was pleased I hadn't burned anything to a crisp.

As I untied my filthy apron, a knock came at my door. I dusted my hands off and abandoned the kitchen left in ruins, eagerly hoping it was Joseph.

I peeked out the peephole and saw him standing in the hallway, his trusty toolbox at his feet. My heart leapt like a gymnast on the pole vault. I ripped open the door and threw my arms around his neck. He staggered back, unprepared for my enthusiastic greeting, and wrapped his arms around me for security.

"Whoa, whoa. Hey there."

I relished the feel of his strong arms around me and savored the smell of his skin. I burrowed my nose along his throat and had no qualms about staying there for the rest of the day.

"I take it you missed me?" The even tone in his voice caught me off guard. His embrace weakened and I slid down his body, a little embarrassed with myself.

I cupped his face and took a long hard look at him. His hair looked like he'd just rolled out of bed. His eyes were heavy and blood shot. And his smile appeared forced and hesitant.

"I'm sorry I practically tackled you. I don't know what came over me."

"Don't be sorry. It was nice to be welcomed home like that for a change." He reached up and dusted the flour from my cheek. "Don't you look cute."

"Yeah, I've been baking all day," I said, brushing some residual flour from his neck.

He sniffed the air. "I can smell it. Apple pie?"

"And cookies," I concluded, rocking back on my heels.

"If it's anything like your lasagna, I know they'll be delicious."

I smiled at his compliment and took his hand. "Come on in and—"

"Actually," he said, picking up his toolbox. "I'd really like to get some sleep. I'm beat."

"Right," I nodded, forgetting about the long hours he spent day after day working on my grandmother's house. "I take it everything's in working order now?"

He ran his hand through his hair, yawning. "Yep. All fixed and up to code. The movers came today too…for your grandmother's bedroom furniture. I helped them load it so they wouldn't scratch it."

"Thank you." I appreciated that more than he'd ever know. I wanted to hug him again, but resisted. For whatever reason, the thought of Caroline popped into my brain and I spoke before I knew what I was saying. "Did you get a chance to talk to Caroline?"

His brows furrowed. "No. I didn't have time. To be honest, I didn't have the energy to deal with her. With everything's that going on, my sister's move, your grandmother's house, Christmas, I put it on the back burner for right now. Sorry, I know that's not what you wanted to hear, but—"

"No, I understand. You've got a lot on your mind."

"Yeah, I do." He started to back away and I panicked. I didn't want him going to sleep thinking I was overbearing. He had always liked the fact that I was independent and didn't throw myself at him.

But I just did.

I felt like I had suddenly made the biggest mistake in our budding relationship and this was Joseph kindly withdrawing from it. I shouldn't have been surprised. I do it all the time. I'm not a serial, ruined-relationship survivor, but a relationship ruiner. Perhaps it was force of habit.

The air around me thinned. The walls closed in and the temperature spiked. Inwardly, I kicked myself, feeling my throat constrict as I drew in calming breaths. I swallowed and played it cool, backpedaling into my apartment. "You get some sleep, and I'll see you tomorrow."

He nodded lethargically and yawned again. "Right. Tomorrow."

With his toolbox dangling from his fingertips, he dragged his boots across the floor and unlocked his door. Without a second glance in my direction, he entered his apartment and shut the door.

I shut mine and collapsed against it. *What was I thinking coming on so strong?* These two weeks of being without him made it easy for me to forget what our relationship was like beforehand. I'd almost forgotten that Joseph and I interacted more like close friends than lovers. We were casual and spontaneous and hardly got hung up on relationship etiquette. We were content to take things as they came and, most importantly, have fun in the process.

So what did I do? I smothered him with affection the minute I saw him. I might as well have cinched a ball and chain around his ankle, for goodness sakes.

Squeezing my eyes shut and feeling a serious headache coming on, I pushed from the door and headed into the kitchen. Nothing helped settle nerves like good old fashion housework. From the looks of the mess in front of me, I should be cool as a cucumber by the time I finished.

As I scrubbed the dishes, I worried I'd overstepped my bounds with Joseph. As I dried them, I fretted over how clingy and pathetic I looked leaping into his arms. As I put them all in the cabinet, I dreaded the thought of him waking up and having second thoughts. I wiped the counter clean and wished I could go back in time and tidy up this mess with one swipe.

For starters, I'd open the door like a normal person and kiss his cheek with a cordial 'hello,' instead of bounding into his personal space the way a WWE wrestler would clothes line his opponent off the ropes. Then, I'd suggest he get some much needed rest. Men loved their sleep and women who insisted they indulge whenever possible. And lastly, I'd have kept my mouth shut about Caroline. Who in their right mind brings up the subject of The Ex, when it was better for both parties to forget she even existed?

As I tried to make sense of my rambling thoughts and suspicions, I came to realize one thing. He didn't forget about her. He basically swept her under the rug. A convenient ploy, it seemed, if he still had feelings for her.

I drummed my fingers on the sanitized counter and ruminated over this revelation. If I had to think about it, Joseph seemed to do this often where Caroline was concerned. Which would explain why she kept creeping back into his life. Whether she was too self-absorbed to recognize she was fighting a losing battle or he felt something for her deep inside, I deserved to know the truth. It wasn't fair for me to be strung along until one of them figured it out.

Straightening my spine, I marched towards the door. He would tell me how he felt about me. I wasn't taking no for an answer either, sleep or no sleep. I yanked open my door and took one step across the threshold. The elevator dinged and the telltale click of what only could be Caroline's Prada heels sounded on the hallway floor.

Chapter Twenty

I shut the door quickly while holding the handle turned, a technique I seemed to have perfected in the past weeks. I held the knob in a tight grip and left the door cracked a little so Caroline wouldn't notice as she walked by. Through the narrow opening, I saw the short black mini dress sashaying at her thighs, most likely a designer label that cost more than my yearly salary. Her expensive French perfume left a trail behind her, assaulting my nose. Her hair cascaded down her back in golden waves and the muscles in her calves flexed with each determined step. This was a woman on a mission.

I swallowed hard and waited as she knocked on his door. Like so many times before, I hated the thought of eavesdropping, but I felt I was left with no alternative. With Caroline making her last stand, it was crucial to my poor heart that I find out just how Joseph felt and how he was going to handle this unexpected situation.

She knocked a second time with more force and I swore I heard her sigh. I laid my ear alongside the crack so I wouldn't miss a single word. My heart thumped in my chest. Joseph's door opened and I held my breath.

"What are you doing here?"

There was little emotion in his voice. Given the flat tone of his greeting, I couldn't tell if he was just groggy from his interrupted nap or perturbed about her wakening him up. I hoped he was glaring at her.

"I wanted to talk," Caroline said sweetly. I should have known the woman was capable of sugaring her voice to that of a delightful person.

"We have nothing to talk about, Caroline. I told you, it's over."

A good start so far. They were through and she couldn't grasp it. I could live with that scenario.

"Joseph, you don't believe that."

"I do."

"You say that now because you're confused."

"Confused?"

I thought the same thing as Joseph. What's to be confused about?

"You don't know what your heart wants," she continued. "And that's not your fault. It's mine. I blamed you for not being there for me, when all along you were. It was I who wasn't there for you. Between my modeling career and traveling to Milan and Paris, I just didn't have the time to devote to you. But now..." I heard her voice escalate, emphasizing the grand finale of her monologue. I imagined her swaying closer to him, batting her lashes, and brushing her long pretty nails down his chest. "Now I do, and I know what it takes to be committed. I'm willing to give you my all, Joseph."

She paused momentarily and brought out all her seductive powers when she ended her speech with one soft, dulcet word. "Everything."

I had to give her credit. She knew what she was doing. She knew exactly what to say to bring a grown man to his knees. I knew what "everything" meant. I could only imagine how often that one little word helped her gain everything she ever wanted.

"Are you finished?" I heard him mumble. My brows rose in curiosity. He didn't sound the least bit interested in her offer.

"Yes, I'm finished. Talking, that is. So, why don't you invite me in and let me—"

"I don't think so," he commanded sternly.

Yes! Thata boy. Tell the conniving wench no. Goodness knows she's never heard that before.

"Caroline, I'm tired—"

"Ah, baby, I can see that," she cooed—with so much pity it was sickening. "You look exhausted."

"No, I'm tired of *this*," he corrected. "I'm tired of your advances. I'm tired of your head games. The way you talk to Jamie...."

"Jamie?"

"Yes, Caroline. You continually cut her down, and she hasn't done anything to you. I don't like it."

I couldn't stop the smile that inched upward on my lips. I loved that my southern gentleman found his backbone and stuck up for me. This was really getting good.

"Fine, baby. I'll apologize to her, if that's what you want."

"Geez, Caroline," he sighed. "You're not listening to me."

I had no idea what he was doing at this moment, but I could just imagine him threading angry hands through his hair. I'd never encountered this side of Joseph, but I had to admit, it was exciting to witness. Especially when I was not on the receiving end of his aggravation.

"I don't want you to apologize to Jamie. In fact, I don't want you to talk to her *at all*! Ever again. Do you understand?"

"I hear you, Joseph," she tried to soothe. I imagined Caroline was getting pretty squirmy. She was losing this game and she knew it. I waited for her to pull out the big guns. "I get it. She's a good friend of yours, and if you and I are to make this work, I have to play nice. I can do that. Whatever it takes."

Holy crap. She was desperate now.

"Joseph, I love you. I always have."

There it was. The love card. She threw it on the table and I held my breath waiting for Joseph to fold. I brought my fingers to my lips and tore the top off a nail. If he didn't soon get rid of her, I'd have the ugliest hands in Cincinnati for Christmas.

"I know you love me."

Was he going to cave? *No! You can't give in to her. Joseph, no! Please don't. Please don't break my heart...*

"And you know I've never been able to reciprocate."

"And that's okay, Joseph. I know you have a difficult time letting your guard down and allowing your heart to feel. But I can wait. I know I said I couldn't, but that was before I really knew what I risked in losing you. I—"

"Caroline." The harsh, unyielding tone of his voice returned. My heart skipped. "I *can't* love you."

"You can if you—"

"I can't. I can't love you because..." His words trailed off and my breath caught. "Because I'm in love with someone else. There I said it. I'm in love."

My mouth dropped wide open. Did I hear him right?

"In love?" Caroline asked. "With who?"

I heard Joseph sigh, but he didn't say a word. Instead, Caroline broke in, exposing her claws.

"Jamie? Next door? That little mousy thing?"

"Lower your voice, Caroline," I heard him scold. "You may think she's mousy, but I think she's the most beautiful woman who ever walked the face of this earth."

Caroline was in as much shock as I was. "Jamie? The Jamie in Loft B, right here." I imagined her pointing her manicured finger down the hall.

"Yes."

My heart soared and every muscle in my body wanted to leap for joy. Trembling with elation, I continued to listen. This was very best day of my life.

"You're sleeping with her, aren't you?"

I wanted to laugh. Caroline couldn't have been more furious with her accusation.

"Actually, no. We haven't even gone there. And I'm fine with that."

I thought back to my college psychology classes. Caroline had one more defense mechanism to go through. She'd already been through the Denial stage and then the Anger stage. All that was left was the Bargaining stage.

"Joseph, sweetie, she can't give you what you need. You're a man and you need a woman who knows exactly how to pleasure the wild animal in you. We both know that's not so easy to do."

She uttered a fake, cutesy giggle. I wanted to vomit.

"Caroline, how do I say this so you'll understand?" I heard him draw in a huge breath. "I don't love you. I never will. We are finished, and there is no hope for us ever getting back together. Ever. I love Jamie and I won't have you ruining the best thing that has ever happened to me. I've tried to be nice about this. I've tried for years to make you understand that I can't fall in love with you. I've changed my locks, for God's sake, and you still can't get it through your thick skull that we're done. Finished. I didn't want to end it this way, Caroline, but you leave me no choice. I want you to walk your little Prada pumps down to that elevator and never come back. If I so much as see your face or even find out you stepped one foot in this apartment complex, I'll call the police."

"You can't be serious, Joseph."

"I've never been more serious in all my life. Goodbye, Caroline." His door closed.

"Mark my words, Joseph, you'll be sorry you ever said goodbye to me."

I don't think so. The only one sorry was Caroline.

I heard her harrumph and stomp down the hall. My heart swelled so much I thought it might burst. Hearing the ding of the elevator was like striking my own exclamation point at the end of *Don't let the door hit you where the good Lord split you*!

I closed my door quietly. In silence, I fist pumped repeatedly and mouthed the words YES! over and over.

He loves me!

Joseph Alexander Scarbrough loved me and told Caroline to kiss his sweet little ass goodbye in the most profound, indisputable way. I twirled and jumped, shimmied and cha-chaed around the room. *I won!* I won the most perfect man in the world and I didn't have to plead, beg, borrow, or steal to get him. He was mine, fair and square. Was this for real?

I panted from the exertion of my spontaneous victory dance and slumped onto my couch and closed my eyes. I sat there giving myself time to let this all sink in.

I was the most beautiful woman to walk the face of this earth.

I was the best thing that had ever happened to him.

He can't love Caroline because he's in love with me. Me!

Me, me, me, me, me!

I wanted to run next door and tackle him with the biggest hug imaginable. I wanted to thank him for kicking Caroline to the curb, once and for all. I wanted to tell him how much I appreciated him. For everything. For being my neighbor. For welcoming me to the building in nothing but a towel. For making me laugh and squishing cupcakes in my face. For risking life and death just to hang Christmas lights in a tree. For helping my grandmother and taking his vacation time to do it. And best of all, for loving me the way no man had ever loved me.

I bolted upright and scavenged my apartment for my cell. I punched in 411 and gave the teleprompter the name Miranda Cromwell, Lexington, Kentucky. I connected to the number specified and paced the floor.

"Hello?"

"Miranda?" My heart was in my throat. "This is Jamie. Joseph's friend—neighbor."

"Oh, yeah. Hi, Jamie. How are you doing? Joseph told me you're coming to my parent's place for Christmas. He's really excited for you to meet everyone."

"I'm excited too. And that's kind of why I'm calling. I want to give Joseph something really special. And you know him better than anyone. So, is there something he's wanting? Maybe something big for the farm? A tractor? I don't know. I was just thinking I could get him something he could use when he buys the farm back from you."

"Well, that's really thoughtful of you, but…"

"But what?"

"Yeah," she said, hesitating. "Joseph broke the news to me the other day that he's not interested in buying the farm back."

"He's not? Why?" I couldn't begin to fathom why. That family farm meant so much to him.

"I don't know. He said it just wasn't in his plans right now."

I stood stunned. For the life of me, I couldn't understand why he'd let this once in a lifetime opportunity slip through his grasp. The last I talked to him, he seemed excited to buy back what Caroline had convinced him to sell.

"Jamie?" she said after a time of silence.

"Yeah. I'm here," I stammered. "I just can't believe this."

"None of us can. We are all so very disappointed."

At that moment, I knew what I had to do. For Joseph. For the man who meant the world to me. I'd give him the one thing that meant the world to him. Our deal of not spending any money on each other's gift be damned. "Miranda," I stated firmly. "Is the farm still up for sale?"

"Kind of. My uncle agreed to buy it as a last resort. He's like my father. He doesn't want the property to go to outside the family."

"Okay, good. Then I want to buy it. For Joseph."

"Jamie…"

I knew she'd try to talk me out of my plan. If our roles were reversed, I'd probably do the same myself.

I straightened my back and dug in. "Just hear me out."

Chapter Twenty-One

It took a long time to convince Miranda that me buying the farm for Joseph was a sensible idea. From the minute she balked, I knew I'd have my work cut out for me, but I pled my case the way a proficient, well-versed defense lawyer would—a regular female Johnnie Cochran. After a grueling debate about what was best for my bank account, the hefty down payment at closing, my insistence that only Joseph's name should appear on the deed, and the fact that he might still refuse to sign despite my generous offer, I had her on board. With the closing date being the day after Valentine's Day, I had my work cut out for me to keep this a secret.

The next morning, though I'd barely got any sleep reeling over my grand scheme, I awoke with a huge smile on my face. Excited to see Joseph's handsome face, I showered and got all dolled up in a shimmery green dress I'd bought from Kohls while he was out of town. Complete with spaghetti straps and a low cut back, I couldn't wait to see the look on his face. I applied a subtle amount of makeup and glittery body cream and finalized my glamorous look with a swipe of Pucker Me Pink lip gloss.

I strapped on a pair of dazzling silver sling-backs and entered the kitchen to begin the day's preparation. With my parents and Grandma coming over around four o'clock, I had some time before I needed to put the ham in the oven. Joseph's whimsical knock resounded upon my door just as I sorted cookies on a tray.

Practically skipping across the room, I ran to open it. I brushed my hands down my dress and gave myself one final check. I bubbled with anticipation and crazy exhilaration and threw open the door.

Joseph stood leaning against the frame in his customary casual stance. He wore a sleek black suit, white shirt, a holly-green tie, and silver cuff links. His unruly lock of hair lay tamed and off his forehead. His face was cleanly shaven, showing off the sharp, strong edges of his jaw and cheekbones. With one hand in the front pocket of his pants, he held a box wrapped in red and green paper, a shiny silver bow topping a cluster of cascading ribbons. To say the least, he looked absolutely dashing and oh so debonair.

His eyes fell over me in the same surprised manner. He drank me in from head to toe, one sparkling fragment at a time.

"Wow," he muttered, shaking his head. "You look…" He swallowed and pushed himself from the door, squaring his shoulders. "…gorgeous," he breathed. "Like Christmas morning."

He reached out and brushed my hair off my shoulders, getting a better look at my outfit. I spun for him, revealing the open back. I heard him groan and his arm snaked around my waist, pulling me against his chest. I felt his warm breath on the back of my neck as he nuzzled my hair.

"You smell just as good as you look."

I giggled when I felt his mouth brush the bare skin on my shoulder. I reached for his face and cupped his smooth cheek. "Merry Christmas, Joseph."

He twirled me back around so I faced him and kissed me softly. "Merry Christmas to you too, Sutherland." He handed me the present and bowed slightly. "And this is for you. But," he added holding it away from me. "I think we should wait until later. When everyone leaves."

The hint of something devilish to come oozed from his statement. I grasped his tie and pulled him back into my arms. "I think that's a great idea." My arms automatically wound around his neck and he tossed the box on the couch to reciprocate the gesture. His grin, absent the dark shadow of scruff that usually accented his lips, knocked me for a loop. I wasn't used to seeing the polished, clean-cut look of my next-door neighbor, slash superintendent, slash boyfriend. He had to be the sexiest man in the universe, and I was the luckiest girl to have all three to myself.

Like the gentleman he was, he stripped off his suit coat and helped me put the seven-pound ham into the oven. We peeled and chopped potatoes, talked about his adventures with helping the moving men load grandma's sleigh bed, laughed like idiots when he didn't notice that the top came off the pepper shaker and dumped a mound of black in the pan, and sneezed the rest of the time scooping it all out.

As we finished preparing the rest of the side items, my family finally showed up. Joseph slipped back into his suit coat before answering the door and, of course, was the crowd-pleaser. Grandma gushed all over again, remarking how he should never hide his handsome face behind all that scruff. Mom gushed too when he complimented her on the scarf she wore, claiming it brought out the youthfulness of her timeless beauty. No surprise that Dad enjoyed Joseph's company, as he finally had someone to talk sports with. Joseph knew as much, if not more than my father, discussing the up and coming talent of the Bengals defense and how the offensive line would be Super Bowl worthy if they had a better quarterback.

The day went off without a hitch, including dinner. Everything turned out edible, as long as you didn't count the unusual spicy flavor of the mashed potatoes. Not much was left of the ham or the rolls, and the apple pie was devoured once I brought out a pot of coffee.

With our stomachs full, we ended the night exchanging gifts. Conversations, laughter, and more stories flew at every turn as each person opened their present. I was especially pleased when Joseph opened his from Grandma. She'd crocheted him a new blue hat, one that rivaled his Montana blue-sky eyes, and when he put it on, she smiled the biggest smile I'd ever seen. My dad was thrilled with his new putter and mom couldn't stop talking about the new laptop Joseph and I picked out. With them moving to Florida, we thought she'd enjoy posting all their beach pictures on Facebook and Skypeing all her close friends back home.

By ten o'clock that night, Dad ushered everyone out the door so they could get an early start on tomorrow's drive to Destin. I hated to see them leave, especially my grandmother, as I had no idea how long it would be before I saw her again. I promised to come down for a visit as soon as spring rolled around, and hugged her tight. Joseph escorted her to the elevator, which again was the highlight of her evening, and reminded my father to call once they made it safely to the Sunshine State. I hugged my family again as the elevator door announced its impatience with repetitive attempts to close and subsequent dings. Eventually, I said my final goodbyes.

The elevator door closed and Joseph turned to me in the hall, snagging my hand.

"That went well," he said, walking me back to my apartment.

"Yes, it did." I looked at him with admiration. That awesome chunk of hair had fallen out of its place. A five o'clock shadow had already started to darken his jaw. The top two buttons of his white dress shirt gaped open and his tie hung loose around his neck. Only Joseph could make unkempt look sexy. I reached up and pulled the knot free, liberating him from the manacles of refinement. "You were a huge hit today."

He pulled me close. "I was, wasn't I?" He kissed my nose. "I think your folks liked me...not as much as your grandmother though."

"There's only one person who likes you more than my grandmother."

He played dumb. "Oh, yeah? Who's that?"

I snuggled into his chest and wrapped my arms around his waist. "Me." I relished the warmth and smell of his skin radiating through his dress shirt. "I adore you, Joseph."

He lifted my chin with his knuckle and gazed into my eyes. The struggle he had for admitting his true feelings was written all over his face, but I didn't mind. I already knew how he felt. Besides, why ruin a good thing with a worn-out phrase?

I stood on my tiptoes and kissed his lips. "You think too much," I quoted him from a few weeks ago. His laughter wrapped around me like a warm snuggly blanket. I didn't think I'd ever tire of it. "Shall we open our presents now?"

He draped his arm over my shoulder and ushered me to the couch. "Good segue."

I sat down beside him and put my gift in his lap. "You're looking at the queen of segues. And sentiment," I added.

"Let's open them at the same time. One two three."

We gave each other curious looks and then dove in. The sound of popping ribbons and shredding paper filled the quiet apartment. At the same time, we both dug into the shroud of tissue paper and held up our gifts. Mine was his UK jersey I'd worn the night of our first official date. Our eyes met and we laughed together, knowing without explanation the sentimentality of that article of clothing.

"I can't believe you gave me your favorite shirt."

"My lucky shirt," he amended. "Besides, it looks much better on you anyway."

"Thank you. And I'm so wearing this to bed tonight." I held it up over my chest and remembered the morning I awoke in his bed wearing nothing but it and a pair of panties.

"You're blushing, Sutherland."

"Am I?"

"Yes, you are." He regarded the terrycloth towel in his lap and ran his fingers across the matching blue stitching. "You put a lot of time in this. Thank you."

"Does that mean I did okay when it came to…how did you put it? Ingenuity?"

He laughed and his eyes sparkled like tinsel on a Christmas tree. "You did just fine. I'm impressed. And grateful." He leaned over and cupped my cheek. "Merry Christmas."

He kissed my lips ever so sweetly and I was lost in the moment. I couldn't believe I had a man as wonderful as this guy. He was selfless, considerate, and so attentive to the things I needed in life without having to be asked. He kept me on my toes with his wit and continually made me laugh. And oh, holy hell could the man rock a suit and tie. How did I ever get so lucky?

When the kiss ended, I melted into him, snuggling into the warmth of his body. He leaned back into the couch and drew me with him. The feel of his sturdy physique offered me the support and comfort I craved after a long day of entertaining. The smell of his skin permeated through his dress shirt and soothed my senses like an effervescent analgesic. I didn't want to let him go.

I heard him sigh and his head drop back against the cushion. "What a day."

I smiled, listening to his even breathing and the rhythmic thump of his heartbeat. He was like a veritable hypnotic audio sleep aid. In this position, I knew I could fall within a few minutes. Somehow I found the will to speak. "This has been the best Christmas ever."

"It ain't over yet, Sutherland. We still have tomorrow."

My smile faded. I was reminded of that old saying: *Every good thing must come to an end*. The last thing I wanted to do was say goodnight to him. My arms automatically tightened around him, holding him captive. I had all I wanted right now in my hands and I didn't want to give it up. It had been the first Christmas where I wasn't alone.

Joseph?"

"Mm-hm?" His chest rumbled like a drowsy bear.

"I don't want you to leave." I said it quickly before I could talk myself out of saying it.

He stirred and brought his arms around me. "I've no intentions of leaving you. I plan on sticking around for a long time. Get used to it."

I smiled. As sweet as it was for him to ease my mind about our future, he didn't understand what I meant. I angled my head to look at him and he peeked at me from beneath closed lids. I touched his face, my heart kicking up speed for what I was about to say. "I mean, I don't want you to leave...tonight." I fidgeted, not knowing how to explain myself without sounding too needy. Too dependent. "I know this sounds stupid, but I don't want to sleep alone, Joseph."

His smile returned and his brow kicked up. "I don't think you should. From experience, if you recall, it gets rather drafty in nothing but a jersey. Assuming you *are* wearing my lucky shirt to bed, I'd be a pretty lame boyfriend to let you freeze to death on Christmas Eve."

I giggled timidly, appreciating his casual, offhandedness. He had such a way of putting my troubled mind at ease without trivializing my concerns.

"Now you go change into that jersey and I'll clean up our mess."

I stood, clutching his shirt against my chest. An image of him whistling at the sight of my bare legs flashed in my insecure brain. "Don't be surprised if I'm under the covers by the time you come in."

"Whatever makes you feel more comfortable." He didn't budge from the couch, but his eyes followed me as I walked toward the bedroom.

Like a skittish colt, I dashed into my bedroom. Heat blazed through my whole body knowing I'd be laying against taut, warm male skin soon. As wonderful as that sounded, I was at such a disadvantage knowing Joseph looked like a Greek god and I, a peasant girl.

I think she's the most beautiful woman who ever walked the face of this earth.

His compliment echoed in my head and I tried to believe it. Trembling, I slipped out of my dress and into his jersey. I could hardly believe what he said about me or that I wasn't going to be sleeping alone at Christmas.

I ran to the bed and yanked the covers down, slipping beneath them. I pulled them up to my chin and nestled down into the crisp, cool sheets. Waiting. Anticipating. Wondering what *he'd* wear to bed. Would he sleep in his dress slacks? *No, too uncomfortable.* Boxer briefs? I could only hope.

It seemed like forever before I heard him moving in the living room. By the sound, I determined he was balling up the tissue and wrapping paper and throwing them in the trash. I heard his footsteps throughout my living space and then dead silence. What was he doing now?

With a casual grace that only Joseph could pull off, he stepped into my room donning nothing but his monogrammed towel. He stood like a tall glass of ice water on a blistering hot day in the dessert. From the first time we'd met, it was like déjà vu all over again. Only this time I wasn't hiding the fact that I stared at him in a towel. I gawked at him like there was no tomorrow.

The man was blessed with long legs, giving him that manly six foot three height. His upper body was hard and lean, the kind of hard a man gets from swinging a hammer and tossing hay bales; not from hours lifting at the gym. His hair was tousled, and the mild shadow of dark, day-old scruff added a hint of bad-boy to his boy-next-door appeal.

"How's it look?" he asked, padding over to my side of the bed as if he were parading down a catwalk. "Does it make my butt look big?"

I laughed aloud at the customary female conundrum he used as a joke. I watched him turn for me and wiggle his cute little tush in the process. "Your butt is perfect. Now, get in here and warm me up. I'm cold."

He held my gaze as he slipped beneath the covers and reclined atop me, his weight pushing me down into the mattress. Unable to breathe, I drowned in those eyes.

Tenderly, he brushed his straight nose along mine and stared back. I could feel our hearts pounding as time stood still for us. So quiet, so close, so…did I dare think it…so in love?

Ever so gradually, he lowered his mouth to mine. The wait was torture, but worth it. I closed my eyes and savored this moment. Our tongues twisted in a slow, erotic dance, and I felt the sensation burn low in my stomach. He tasted of cinnamon and coffee and Joseph, my three favorite things. If we kept this up, I was pretty sure something else would land on my favorites list.

He smiled and rolled to his back, pulling me with him. I looked at Joseph lying on my pillow, a smug little smile adorning his lips. "How can you do that?"

He tucked one hand behind his head, his bicep bulging. "Do what?"

"Just stop and smile like you're happy…and not be…"

"Sexually frustrated?" he finished for me.

I laughed at his ability to put it so frankly. "Yeah. Aren't you the least bit upset that you're lying in my bed and—"

"Jamie," he said, cutting me off. "I'm not upset. I'm not anything. And I sure as heck ain't anything like your asshole boyfriends who made you think sex is the only way for a relationship to work. It's obvious you're not ready or you would've initiated it." He caressed my cheek with the back of his hand. "I'm not going anywhere, Sutherland. Even if it takes weeks, months—years. I'm still going to be here. You're living proof that good things come to those who wait, and I've got all the time in the world for you. We've taken baby steps to get where we are, and I'm totally fine with that. When you're ready, I'll be here."

"You're amazing."

"Yeah, yeah," he said, putting me in a headlock. "Close your eyes and get some sleep."

I laid my head on the smooth, hot skin of his chest and snuggled into his arms. I laid there with the biggest smile on my face. "Joseph?"

"Hmm?"

I circled his nipple with my finger. "Remember when we spent the night at your sister's and I woke up in your bed?"

"Yeah."

The deep sound of his one word reply rumbled in his chest. "Were you sexually frustrated then too?"

His laughter shook my whole head. "Shut up and go to sleep, Sutherland."

Chapter Twenty-Two

I opened my eyes the next morning to the sight of Joseph sleeping next to me. I had to blink several times before I realized I wasn't dreaming. He lay there, so innocent, so peaceful. I hadn't the heart to wake him.

This was a dream come true for me. Sure, I'd done this once before with him, but the last time I was so distraught over the fact that I found him in my arms that I couldn't appreciate the moment.

This morning was way better. We'd planned it. No surprises. And I felt like a woman who had nothing to fear. My life was perfect with him in it.

I stared at him, taking advantage of the opportunity to admire him at such close quarters. He had long lashes for a guy, dark ones that curled up slightly on the tips. He had tiny pores and a clear complexion, probably the result of regimented washing and good facial products passed down from his sisters. His lips were an attractive shade of rose, but not too pink, kissable even as he slept. Everything about his face was absolutely perfect. Even the tiny scar above his left brow couldn't mar his looks. If anything, the blemish gave him character, a flaw that proved he was human after all.

I reached up and caressed the rough whiskers on his face. He stirred and I stopped, waiting for him to settle back into his dreams. I hoped they were of me.

Slipping from beneath the heavy weight of his arm, I sneaked out of bed and tiptoed to the bathroom to shower. I wanted to make a good impression on his parents. I already had the advantage of not being Caroline in my favor, but I also wanted Joseph to be proud of the woman he was falling in love with.

The incredible thought buzzed in my head. Joseph...falling in love. With me.

I could turn a cartwheel right now.

In the span of an hour, I showered and brushed my teeth, dressed in another fancy outfit that would match the heels Joseph seemed so fond of, and curled my hair. After applying a little makeup, I padded back into the bedroom and stopped dead in my tracks.

Joseph, with his back to me, was climbing out of bed, his glorious naked backside as visible as a winter moon on a clear midnight sky. He stretched and the muscles in his back and tush flexed in the most alluring way. He turned to retrieve the towel that had come off amid the tangle of sheets, and saw me.

"So sorry." I turned my head and rotated like a top. I could feel my face burning. "I didn't realize you were awake."

He laughed in his cute, casual way. "Sorry, I thought you were still getting ready."

I didn't dare peek over my shoulder. "I can get your pants for you."

"I'm good. Just had to find the towel and put it back on. Must have come off in the night."

I wish I'd have known that when I woke up.

He came up behind me and whirled me around, pulling me into his arms. He kissed me on the forehead and ran his hand down my hair. "Good morning, Sutherland. Don't you look nice?" I watched him step in front of the bathroom mirror and run his fingers through his hair. He looked himself over, checking the shadow of scruff on his face. "Should I shave?"

"Who you looking to impress by shaving? Candace?"

"Right." He rubbed a hand over his whiskers. "I'd rather impress you."

"Then leave it."

He smiled wickedly at me. "Scruff it is, then. Do you mind if I take a shower here?"

"Knock yourself out. I'll even run next door and get a change of clothes for you, if you want."

"Thanks. Just jeans and a dress shirt, though. Bottom drawer."

I crossed my arms. "You going commando?"

His laughter echoed against my bathroom walls. "Hardly. Second drawer from the top. And a toothbrush, if you don't mind."

"Okay. I'm on it." I snagged his key from the bedside table and left him to get ready. I started the coffee pot, and then skipped next door to his apartment. It was the first time I used key since he gave it to me. I felt empowered.

Flipping on the lights, I closed the door behind me and gazed around his home. The natural scent of Joseph surrounded me. How happy it made me to breathe it in and let my senses indulge.

As I walked to his bedroom, THE photo album caught my eye. Like the last time I was in here, it sat on his coffee table, begging me to take a peek. I bit my lip. What would it hurt?

I walked over and picked it up. *Just a quick look.* I braced myself to see Caroline's Barbie Doll face. Not exactly the way I'd choose to start my day but such are the wages of sin. I flipped the cover open. But it wasn't Caroline I saw on the first page. It was a woman I'd never seen before. A young twenty-something with Joseph's Montana blue-sky eyes and his straight as an arrow nose. Her arm draped around Joseph's shoulder and they both looked so happy in this picture. I guessed that I was looking at Lindsey.

I flipped the next page. Lindsey again. This time on the back of a horse.

Next page. Lindsey on the beach, buried in the sand with a nice pair of sand-mound breasts someone had shaped for her. I laughed and turned the next page. Lindsey with a pair of thick-lensed glasses, her eyes the size of saucers. There was a caption below that read, "Look! You can hear me blink!"

I cracked up as I could actually hear the blink-blink sound effect of a cartoon character blinking. I loved this woman. I couldn't stop. I flipped through the next pages.

Lindsey and Joseph swinging from the tree house rope out into the lake.

Lindsey, Miranda, and Candace, and what I believed to be a six-year old version of Evelyn, Miranda's daughter, holding paint brushes and wearing handkerchiefs on their head. Paint splatters and swatches in pink and yellow randomly covered their faces, as if they'd spent more time painting each other than the walls.

Next page: Lindsey, wearing an elegant long red dress, in the arms of a handsome fellow, whom I assumed to be her high school prom date. The next page displayed yet another prom date picture, this time in a sparkly blue dress, with a more dramatic pose than the first.

I studied each picture, my heart melting with every single one. The fact that Joseph had a collection of photos, documenting the memories of his sister, had me admiring him that much more.

I turned over the last page of the album. There were the photo booth pictures from our Kenwood Mall shopping extravaganza. My breath caught and my knees went weak. I had to sit. I wasn't strong enough to take this standing up. I felt so special to have been added to his book of treasured memories.

I closed the album, hot tears burning my eyes. I had suspected Caroline occupied these pages, when all along it was his family. The people he loved and cherished. And I was in there.

I placed the book back where it belonged and walked to his bedroom. As I retrieved his jeans, shirt, and boxer briefs from the chest of drawers, I pondered my impulsive decision to buy the farm back for Joseph. If I had any doubts, they were totally gone now.

Joseph's heart was the size of Texas, and I'd be damned if I'd give him any less. He deserved to know what unselfish love was. To know it's possible to be loved unconditionally without expecting a thing in return. Love was not about finding that perfect someone who makes you happy—but rather it was getting lost in the pursuit of that person's happiness with no regard for your own.

Joseph taught me that. He made me realize love wasn't a destination, but a journey. A voyage of baby steps and the commitment of cherishing the now along the way. At any moment, that precious 'now' could be ripped from our hands. I only had to look at the pictures of Lindsey to know how quickly life can change.

I loved Joseph. I knew that now with every breath I took, but words were inadequate and most times useless. Joseph and I both had grown to detest those three, little, threadbare words, because of the pathetic people in our past. And although I might not be able to voice my love for him now, come February—if I could hold out that long—I'd give my heart to him the way Joseph was sure to understand.

* * * *

Christmas at his folk's place was like nothing I could've ever imagined. It was loud the minute Joseph and I walked through their door, the whole place full of excitement, laughter and conversation. Candace waved from the living room, the impersonal greeting I half expected from her, and went back to yelling at the basketball game on TV. Evelyn sat next to her, her nose in an iPhone, texting, until the second she saw Joseph. Her eyes lit up and she came rushing toward him, throwing her arms around his waist. I saw the love on his face as he hugged her back. Kissing the top of her head, he introduced her as his favorite niece.

"I'm your only niece, Uncle Joseph," she quipped back.

Out of nowhere, Miranda's twin boys ran around my legs. Spencer, their father, said a quick 'hello' and chased after them while Joseph embraced his sister.

"I thought you said you wouldn't be here for Christmas, Randi."

"I thought so too, but Spencer insisted we fly back for the holiday." She watched her husband headlock one son and tickle the other. "Guys, seriously. Settle down."

"Oh, they're fine," Joseph's mother said, coming around the corner. "And you must be Jamie." I balanced the apple pie I'd brought in one hand and held out my other to shake hers. She dismissed it and pulled me into a tight hug. "Shaking hands is for stuffy old men."

Joseph's mother was taller than me by a few inches. She carried herself with poise and grace without being too rigid. Her perfume was subtle and not outdated like so many woman wore at her age. She was probably the most beautiful sixty-year-old woman I'd ever seen. I imagined she was a blonde bombshell in her younger years.

She accepted my dessert and smiled warmly. "Aren't you just a pretty little thing? I love that dress, Jamie. And those heels. You have remarkable taste, my dear."

"Thank you, Mrs. Scarbrough." Like Joseph, his mother was easy to warm up to, unlike Candace, who obviously didn't take after the maternal side of the family. I could tell Mom and I would get along just fine.

"Joseph." I could hear the love in Mrs. Scarbrough's voice as she hugged him. "Merry Christmas, darling."

"Merry Christmas, Mom. Where's Dad?"

"In here!" Mr. Scarbrough called from the kitchen. "Your mother's got me slicing this damn ham. I'm missing the game!"

Mrs. Scarbrough rolled her eyes. "Joseph, why don't you help him before he drops it on the floor."

Joseph called his two nephews, and told them if they hauled all the presents in from his truck, they'd get to open theirs first. Spencer followed the rambunctious boys outside to make sure they didn't drop or break any and

Miranda took my coat. In no time, I was inducted into the Scarbrough house of chaos.

While Joseph and his father tended the roast, Miranda and I assisted Mrs. Scarbrough in setting the table. Amid the clatter and clinks of the china, Christmas music played in the background, and shouts of disgust erupted at intermittent times from the televised NBA game. It was a holiday get together unlike anything I'd ever witnessed. With sports actually allowed in the house, my father would feel right at home here.

I couldn't help but take in all the pandemonium; the boisterous chatter, the hearty laughter, and the way everyone in this family spoke over each other. Aside from Mrs. Scarbrough—and Evelyn, whose whole world lay in the palm of her hand (literally)—their voices carried from room to room. It amazed me how anyone could concentrate with so many conversations going on at one time.

By the end of dinner, I'd gotten used to the racket, and I no longer flinched at sudden loud noises. Having everyone jammed into one room, around one long table, cured that mighty quick. Not long after we ate, I began collecting dirty dishes and washed them by hand. Miranda joined in, while Candace and her father, still absorbed with the Knicks game, made their way back into the living room.

Though I knew Joseph would've liked to watch the game, he commandeered Henry and Hunter, giving Spencer a break. He chucked them over his shoulder and marched around for effect. I heard giggles and growls resounding as he played something akin to Conan the Barbarian, body-slamming them on the couch beside Candace. I stifled a laugh as she socked him in the arm.

Miranda reached across me for one of the dishes I'd rinsed and toweled it dry. "You doing all right?" she asked, ignoring the pile up session her twins had initiated upon Joseph's back.

"Yeah, I'm great." Joseph shouted a fake cry for help from all fours as the boys clung to him like rabid spider monkeys. "You're kids are sure—"

"A pain in the ass, I know," Miranda said, shaking her head.

"I was going to say having fun," I corrected politely, taking notice of Joseph's hearty laughter as the twins rode him like a horse. "But I think someone else is enjoying himself more."

Miranda smiled. "Yeah, Joseph's great with the boys. Always has been. He'll make a great father one day."

Miranda's statement hung in the air and I wasn't certain how to respond. I'd not given thought to Joseph having kids, or actually to me having *his* kids, especially this soon in our relationship. But the thought now tingled in my brain.

For the first time in my life, I could actually see myself wanting kids, wanting to do more than just nurture a coffee shop from a one-bedroom apartment in the city. And if Joseph were the father, I'd be even more interested. *Baby steps, Sutherland,* I could hear him say.

"So," Miranda finally said. "What did you finally decide to get for Joseph for Christmas?"

I laughed nervously. "Well, we made a deal not to spend money on each other. Our gifts were supposed to be something we already owned and wanted the other to have."

"Oh yeah? That sounds like Joseph. Very noncommittal."

"Actually, I liked the idea," I said without going into much detail. "It relieved a lot of unnecessary pressure, you know."

"Sure. So, what was the present of choice?"

I think I blushed a little. "I gave him a towel. With his initials embroidered on it." She looked at me oddly and I suddenly felt the need to elaborate a little. "That's how we met. He was wearing nothing but a towel."

"Really?" she asked, drying another dish. "But I thought you guys met in the hallway of your apartment?"

"We did. But..."

"I don't think I want to know the rest," she said cringing. "And he gave you?"

"His UK jersey."

Her mouth dropped a little and her eyes widened. "His jersey? The one with the number thirty-three on it?"

"Yeah. Why?"

A curious smile quirked up on her lips. "You do know the importance of that number, don't you?"

I bit my lip. "No."

She came closer to me and spoke low. "That's Lindsey's number."

"Oh." The word came out as a muffled realization, for words utterly failed me.

"See, Lindsey used to play fast-pitched softball in high school and she won all kinds of awards. Broke lots of records. I think some of her records still stand for the state of Kentucky. Anyway..." She looked over her shoulder to make sure Joseph couldn't hear. "The school retired her number and held a huge ceremony. It was a big deal for all of us. Not long after that, Joseph was at a UK game and bought a jersey with her number on it. He wore it all the time."

I stood stunned. I had no idea that the sentiment of that jersey went beyond being a UK fan. I glanced down at the soap bubbles, pondering all the new facets of Joseph's character. This was a man who wasn't in the least one dimensional. There were so many sides to him, as unpredictable as they were fascinating, and each time I discovered a new one, I fell that much harder for him.

Miranda nonchalantly bumped my elbow to gain my attention. "I know it's not exactly as profound as an engagement ring, but that's a big leap for Joseph."

"Right. Right," I uttered, overwhelmed by this news.

"Hey," she said, touching my arm. "This is a good thing. For you, especially." She squeezed my forearm and smiled. "Joseph would never part with that jersey unless..."

I hung on her last words, waiting for her finish, but Evelyn came rushing up beside us, her phone in her hand.

"Mom, Samantha said I could spend the night at her house tonight. Can I? Please?"

Miranda struggled to composed herself, blindsided by the interruption of her daughter's question. She stammered as she gazed at me.

"Please, Mom...she's my best friend. One last time before we have to leave for Denver tomorrow?"

She smiled and gave in. "Sure, honey. Tell her we'll drop you off in a little while. After presents though."

Evelyn kissed her mom on the cheek. "Thanks, Mom. You're the best!" She skipped out of the kitchen, texting as she plopped on the couch next to Candace.

"I'm sorry," Miranda apologized. "Where were we?"

I looked at Joseph, who taunted Candace with a piece of mistletoe he'd just pulled from his pocket, and laughed. I didn't feel the need to delve back into the conversation. I understood the significance of his gift without Miranda having to spell it out for me. I hugged her and whispered in her ear. "I treasure everything your brother has given me, the best being his heart. I won't break it. I promise."

She hugged me back and I could feel her body trembling a little when she did so. I'm sure a lot of it was due to the loss of her sister. Holidays always made the loss of someone we love so much more poignant. I couldn't imagine the void Lindsey's passing left in this family's world. But also knowing Miranda was a mother hen in every sense of the word meant she wanted the best for her little brother, especially since he'd been hurt before.

She pulled away and wiped her tears before they could be seen. "I didn't mean to push all that on you, Jamie," she whispered. "I just wanted you to know how Joseph feels...in case you were having second thoughts about buying the farm for him and all."

"No," I insisted, taking hold of her hand. "I'm not having second thoughts. In fact, I feel you should know that I want nothing but the very best for Joseph. I'd give him the whole world, if I could."

She glanced over at Joseph. "I haven't seen him smile this much in years. I think you already have, Jamie."

Chapter Twenty-Three

A month and a half later

February 14th. A Tuesday. A world-renowned feast day. A Hallmark holiday for some. But for me, it was a dedicated, heart-doodled square on my desk calendar, depicting a date for which I'd been waiting so long. I Xed out the space and smiled. Today was Valentine's Day and the night I would give Joseph the world. Well, at least twenty acres of it.

We'd planned to go to dinner after I closed the coffee shop, where—I had no idea because he said it was a surprise—and then we'd head to some charming bed and breakfast place he found near Lexington. It went without saying how excited I was, but for multiple reasons.

One: To see the look on his face when I presented him with the check that would make his dreams come true.

And two: To spend some quality time with him after so many weeks of being without him. Once Christmas and New Year's passed, we hardly saw each other except on weekends. Our work schedules had conflicted, and when he wasn't working long hours on some tenant's clogged drain or retiling a floor, he was often traveling to his family's farm to help Candace with the horses.

Any other woman might suspect a lover on the side. I knew better, however. Joseph was a lot of things, but not a liar or a cheat. I no longer suspected the worst or drew up cynical scenarios of how his feelings for me would eventually fizzle. I'd known from past experience how exhausting those thoughts could be. The strain of suspicion alone had ended many of my otherwise healthy relationships. Because of Joseph, I was over that way of thinking. Totally liberated.

At six-forty-five, I poked my head out of my office and caught Melissa's smile as she rang up a group of customers. "Get ready, Jamie. I got this."

I loved that Melissa shared my excitement. It seemed we both lived vicariously through each other.

I closed my office door and kicked off my shoes. I untied my apron and hung it on the back of the door. Digging into my duffle bag, I pulled out a change of clothes. Joseph and I made a deal not to get all dressed up, so I pulled on a pair of jeans and a pretty blue and white sweater. I released my hair from its ponytail holder, shook it out and gathered the majority of it back into a relaxed bun, letting a few loose strands frame my face. I freshened up my makeup and slipped into my favorite pair of knee-high, leather boots. After swiping some gloss across my lips, I was ready for my date.

With a few minutes to spare, I slid behind my desk again and made some last minute scheduling changes. Hearing the door chimes and Melissa bidding the last patron farewell, I prepared for her to slide into my office like Cosmo Kramer in an old Seinfeld episode.

Like I predicted, her entrance was anything but subtle. The door swung open, hitting the wall with a thud. Melissa's hand was still attached to the doorknob though so she smacked into the door too. She grinned at me. "What time is Joseph coming to pick you up?"

I checked the clock on the wall. "Any minute now."

She sauntered up to my desk and sat on its edge. "Is tonight *the* night?" She wagged her eyebrows, indicating there was more to our date than just a good meal.

I bit my lip. "Maybe."

She whipped a dishrag at me. "Oh, come on! Don't you think it's time already? Geez Jamie, how long are you going to make the poor man wait? You've been dating for over three months. If that hunk of manhood was mine, I'd have jumped his bones the first chance I got."

"It's not something you plan."

"Hello!" she sang out. "Yes, it is!"

I tapped my pen on the table. "I don't know. I prefer spontaneity."

She scoffed. "Even spontaneity requires a little planning, Jamett Penelope Sutherland. Tell me you at least shaved your legs."

I laughed. "Yes, I shaved my legs."

"Thata girl." She jumped to her feet and danced around my office, singing her words as if they were from an actual song. "Oh my gosh, I've waited so long for this…I can't wait to hear how things go tonight…It's going to be amazing…" She stopped in her tracks. "You better call me first thing in the morning."

I thought about the extensive preparations I'd made for this night, despite denying so with Melissa. I'd bought two cupcakes from the bakery that Joseph liked so much and placed them in a box with red ribbons and hearts. Beneath my jeans and sweater, I wore the sexiest, laciest, reddest lingerie ensemble I could find at Victoria Secret. I hoped he'd take so much great pleasure in unwrapping both gifts that it took all night.

"How about first thing in the *afternoon*?" I bartered.

She growled a wicked laugh. "Oooo, you naughty girl. Even better." She gasped and looked toward the café. "He's here!" If it wasn't for Melissa's supersonic hearing, I wouldn't have known Joseph had showed up. "Hurry, Jamie!" she called, ushering me out of the office with my coat, purse, and gift.

I could see Joseph through the tall, plate glass windows. My heart skipped. He wore his Carhartt coat, a pair of jeans, boots, and a white button-up shirt. His face was full of scruff, his bright smile meeting his eyes. I melted.

I unlocked the door and let him in. The cold winter wind rushed in behind him. His hands reached for my elbows and he kissed me gently, avoiding the gift box in my grasp. "Hi there, Sunshine."

"Hi." A squeal escaped me. I didn't mean to sound so giddy, but I was. So was Melissa as she uttered an empathetic "awwww."

We both smiled at her and stood in front of each other in awkward silence.

"So," he finally said. "You ready to go?"

My stomach somersaulted. "Yes." I looked toward Melissa. "Are you okay locking up?"

"I'm fine. Now, you two kids run along and have fun," she said, pushing us both out the door. "And don't forget to call me, Jamie."

She and Joseph exchanged peculiar looks. Something was definitely up between them, but the moment Joseph's hand touched the small of my back as he opened the door to his truck for me, I became incapable of coherent thought. Even through the thickness of my coat, I could feel the sweet intimacy of his touch. How would I feel later when we didn't have the separation of clothing between us? The blush that started on my cheeks traveled all the way to my toes.

From the passenger seat, I watched him shut my door and circle the vehicle. He climbed inside next to me, and I couldn't help but notice the look of anticipation on his face. He smiled as he turned the key, the engine roaring to life.

"You look beautiful, Sutherland."

"Thank you."

He checked his side-view mirror for oncoming cars and pulled out. We left Cincinnati behind and drove south to Lexington, talking about our hectic work week. That was one thing I loved about our relationship. We never seemed to run out of things to talk about and when I spoke, he listened as if everything I had to say was of the utmost importance.

As we neared Lexington, I noticed Joseph got strangely quiet as I rambled about Grandma and all the fun she was having in Florida with my parents.

"Sorry I'm talking so much. I'm just thrilled she's enjoying the sunshine and the beach. Mom's even got her wading in the ocean, which is huge, because Grandma doesn't swim."

"We should schedule a surprise visit soon. Don't you think?"

"We?" I asked, liking the sound of us taking a vacation together.

"Sure, why not? I bet your grandmother would love to see you."

"She'd probably enjoy seeing you more." I imagined Joseph in his swim trunks, his tan bare chest glistening in the hot sun, and I knew Grandma wouldn't be the only person enjoying his visit.

"We're almost there," he said turning off the freeway at the Georgetown exit. I racked my brain for what fancy restaurant he was taking me to. He reached behind the seat and pulled out a blindfold. "Here, put this on."

I looked at the satiny red material in his hand. "What's this for, Mr. Christian Grey?"

He chuckled. "Don't worry, there's no Red Room of Pain where we're going. Just put it on and savor the anticipation."

I did as he asked, my head spinning. Did he intend for me to be blindfolded for most of the evening? I bit my lip. I'd never done anything like this before. Was he the kind of guy who liked to spice things up on a regular basis? With Joseph, I wouldn't be opposed to a little kink.

"You can't see anything, can you?"

His deep voice sounded so erotic from behind the blindfold that I felt it everywhere. I finally understood why blindfolds were so popular among couples. "Not a thing."

I felt his hand take hold of mine, and I relished the warmth and strength of his grasp as he spoke to me. "I hope you don't mind, but I decided instead of going to dinner at a crowded restaurant, we're going to order take-out from the bed and breakfast. Does that sound good to you?"

The thought of being totally alone with Joseph sounded more than good. Blindfolded and alone with Joseph sounded even better. "I'm game for whatever you have in mind."

I heard Joseph clear his throat, the kind of sound that defined exactly what he was thinking. Not too much longer now and I'd know for sure.

As I sat in total darkness during the rest of the drive to the B&B, my other senses kicked in and I could smell him now more than ever. I couldn't wait to get there and bury my nose in his neck. I imagined slow dancing with him and breathing in the scent of his warm skin and cologne as we waited for dinner to be delivered.

I heard him downshift and felt the truck veer to the right. In a short distance, we turned again and I could tell we were climbing a small hill. He slowed the vehicle to a halt and killed the engine.

"Keep that blindfold on, you hear? I'm serious, Jamie. Don't peek or you'll ruin my surprise."

What kind of surprise? I couldn't imagine what he had planned and the last thing I wanted to do was ruin it. "I won't. Scouts honor."

"Good. Sit tight for a second." I heard his truck door open and shut, and felt the rocking of the vehicle as he slid to the ground. His boots sounded along the paved ground, growing more distant with each step he took. I listened closely. Where in heck could we be?

Again I heard his boots, this time coming back toward the truck. The shuffle of heavy fabric surrounded me in the cab and the truck rocked momentarily again. What was he doing now?

Finally, the driver's side door opened and I felt him slip back inside. I jumped as he slammed it shut, the smell of my handsome, mysterious Joseph tingling my senses.

"Okay, you can take off the blindfold now." I felt his hand on my leg. A jolt of warmth raced through me like an electric current. I almost didn't want to rid myself of the blindfold.

I reached up and pulled it off anyway. The cab of the truck was pitch black. I realized he'd blanketed the vehicle with a canvas cover.

He clicked on an LED lantern and placed it on the floorboard. He sat facing me, a small rectangular gift box in his hand. "Let's play truth or dare. Here's the truth."

I took the box from him, my eyes glued to the pair of pink and purple bows topping it. "We're going to open our gifts in here? In the truck?" I thought about my gift and how I intended to give it to him in a more romantic setting.

"*You* are," he said complacently.

"But why in here? And what's with the cover?"

"Will you quit asking so many questions and just open your gift."

I bit my lip again, enjoying his little game. "Fine. I'll open it." I lifted the lid of the dainty present and inside lay a fortune cookie (should've expected that) and a skeleton key with a purple satin ribbon tied to it. A tiny memory from my childhood filtered in when I'd imagined inserting this very skeleton key into a lock below the crystal knob on my grandmother's bedroom door. At the tender age of four, I'd pretended I was a beautiful princess living in a grand Victorian mansion where Grandma and I would have tea and crumpets like the English aristocracy.

"Do you know what that is?" he asked.

I picked it up and admired the nostalgic Colonial design of the vintage pewter key. "This is a key to my grandmother's bedroom. Does she know you have this? And why are you giving it to me?"

"The truth is in the fortune cookie."

I looked at the key again. I had no idea what Joseph was up to. And whatever it was, what did this key have to do with it? I cracked open the cookie and unfolded the little slip of paper inside. I read the words to myself and I smiled like I'd been given a five carat diamond ring. It read:

I LOVE YOU A LATTE

Seeing his heart and soul spelled out on a cookie fortune almost meant more to me than hearing it from his lips. Almost.

I flipped it over and read the back. I froze. I read it again, then looked at him. "Why is my grandmother's address written on this fortune?"

"Because it's yours now."

I didn't think I heard him right. "I don't understand, Joseph."

He opened his truck door and squeezed out, jerking the car cover off the cab. Lit up before me was my grandmother's house. I recognized it instantly, but it wasn't the same. The color of the siding was no longer pale blue, but a light mocha. The tin roof was a deep chocolate brown, swirling like Hershey's syrup around the single dormer window above the porch. Crisp white bargeboard trimmed the gable roofs and fancy, white-washed spindles and railings sectioned off a charming sitting area filled with white wicker furniture with brown and pink paisley cushions. Above that, hung a huge sign that read *I LOVE YOU A LATTE Bed & Breakfast and Coffee Shop*.

I felt a painfully-sweet tightness in my chest as I stared through his windshield at the magnificent view before me. My eyes burned with tears. I brought my hand up to my mouth to keep my chin from shaking.

Joseph opened my door and bowed like a gentleman, holding out his hand for me. "M'lady."

I laid my hand in his. I bit my lip to control its trembling. I could hardly speak, much less move. "Is this…?"

"It's all yours, Sutherland. I bought it from your grandmother before she left for Florida."

I gawked at him, unable to process this staggering revelation.

He reached in, lifted me from the truck seat, and carried me toward the house. I couldn't stop staring at it as I held on to him.

"You bought my grandmother's house?"

"And renovated it to be a Bed & Breakfast slash coffee shop. What do you think?"

Tears ran down my cheeks and my chin quivered. I was so overwhelmed with emotion I could barely think at all. Joseph Scarbrough had bought my grandmother's house for me and turned it into the most beautiful Victorian Bed & Breakfast I'd ever seen. But how? How did he do all this without me knowing? "When did you…"

He carried me up the porch steps and sat me on one of the chairs, taking a seat beside me. The sharp smell of paint and brand new patio cushions wafted around me.

He took my hand. "Do you remember when I took two weeks of vacation to help your grandmother fix a few things?"

"Yes…"

"And lately, when I said I was helping my sister with the horses? Well, I wasn't. I was here, renovating, painting, knocking down walls and opening up rooms. Sanding hardwood floors and building cabinets. I didn't think I was going to get it finished for Valentine's Day, but I did." He paused and inched his bottom off the edge of the seat, his face serious. "I wanted to surprise you, Jamie, especially after it broke your heart that she was selling. And, of course, once I told your grandmother what my intentions were, she practically moved heaven and earth to get the paperwork going. I hope you can forgive me for lying to you."

A laugh escaped me despite the tears pouring from my eyes. "Forgive you? Forgiving you is easy, Joseph. It's making sure you understand my deepest appreciation that's going to be impossible. I have no words to tell you how grateful I am that you did this for me. That you thought enough of me to spend all your hard-earned—"

I stopped midsentence, suddenly realizing why he passed up the opportunity to buy his farm back. All his funds had gone to purchasing and renovating my grandmother's house. "But what about your farm, Joseph? You—"

"That farm will have to wait. This was more important. You…" he paused a moment, "…are more important." He reached up and caressed my wet cheek with his thumb. "Making you smile…that's what means the world to me, Jamie. Besides, my uncle is buying the farm tomorrow, and he said if I ever decided I was ready, I could buy it back from him. So all's not lost."

I wasn't sure what was more profound. The fact that Joseph bought my grandmother's house for me as a surprise or that I was about to buy his farm for him. "Joseph, I need to tell you something."

He stood and pulled me to my feet with him. "It'll have to wait. Right now, I want to show you the inside. Come on."

His childlike eagerness was adorable. He unlocked the front door and held it open for me. "Welcome to *I LOVE YOU A LATTE Bed & Breakfast and Coffee Shop.*"

I stepped inside, my gaze taking in everything brand new that mingled with the old and familiar. The walls looked revitalized and clean with a fresh coat of paint, while my grandmother's accent pictures still remained where they had always hung. I was glad to see he kept the old woodwork, but what was once dark and dreary, now trimmed each room with bright white modern appeal. Grandma's furniture and antique collections sat proudly in the renovated spaces, maintaining their lovely vintage charm on the refinished hardwood floor.

I stood in awe of Joseph's hard work and craftsmanship. "I can't believe what you've done to this place."

"I tried my best to liven up the house without removing the things that gave it its warmth and nostalgia." He turned me around to face the stairs and helped me out of my coat, hanging it on Grandma's coat rack beside the door. "For instance, your grandmother's phone table. I kept it and the stained-glass lamp, she said you loved so much, against the stair wall. It's behind the new counter I built where your customers will check in and order their coffee, but at least, it's there for you to use at your discretion."

I remembered as a child thinking what an elegant little nook my grandmother had set up against the wall beneath the stairs. I thought I was hot stuff the first time I sat in that chair as a child and made a phone call to my parents while they were on vacation. With everyone converting to cordless phones, I thought it was the neatest thing to be forced to sit in one place and have a conversation. Who knew I'd be using this phone table as an adult? I grabbed his hand and gave it a squeeze, words failing me.

"And upstairs," he said pulling me along, "I left your childhood room as is, save for a new paint job." I peeked in and smiled. My old room looked much larger with the lighter color of paint brightening the walls.

"And the other room up here," he said, leading me down the short hall. "I had to make a few minor adjustments to accommodate the addition of another room. I built a new wall here, and moved the original door down. Now there are two doors and two separate rooms, but..." he added, stepping in and opening yet another door. "The rooms can be contiguous, if the customers prefer adjoining rooms. Good?"

I couldn't stop smiling. "It's fabulous, Joseph."

"I still have a little more to do in the kitchen," he said, leading me back downstairs. "Everything's been rewired to code for the coffee shop, but I figured I'd let you pick out the machines you wanted since you're more educated in that field." Pointing to various things, he continued. "I left your grandmother's table and hutch, and since she had so many assorted coffee cups and saucers, I thought perhaps you might actually use them instead of those Styrofoam cups you have now. Unless of course the customers want their coffee to go, then you might want to have both. Your call. Sound good so far?"

I hardly had time to respond before he led me down the back hall to the bathroom. "Again, here, I repainted, fixed the leaky toilet, and tore out the floor. The old one had some water damage, so I laid a new subfloor and tiled it. I wasn't sure on the color though."

His choice of tile and the matching grout looked perfect. *Everything* was perfect, as far as I was concerned. I couldn't believe the amount of work Joseph had done in such a short amount of time. "Joseph, you did an amazing—"

"Wait, you haven't seen the best part yet. The grand finale!" He led me to my grandmother's bedroom door and gestured toward the crystal knob. "I believe you'll need that key."

I almost forgot I still had it. I stepped toward the door and inserted the skeleton key, the blunt edges of the beautiful crystal knob pressing into my palm. I opened the door and sucked in a huge breath at the beautiful transformation of the room.

An enormous, intricately carved, Victorian sleigh bed with a rich chestnut finish sat in the center of the room. A matching armoire and chest of drawers stood on either side of the bed and one of my grandmother's handmade quilts draped over the king-sized mattress. Coordinating pillows of black velvet and white satin perched at the headboard, while two stained-glass lamps embellished a pair of bedside tables. Victorian-style drapes with tiebacks and tassels hung on the windows. It was the most remarkable replication of French-inspired elegance.

"What do you think?"

I could hear the uncertainty in his voice, but I couldn't speak. Nothing I could possibly say would ever express my true feelings for the hard work and careful consideration Joseph had put into this project. I turned and threw my arms around his neck and sobbed. "Oh, Joseph."

"Hey, there" I heard him say, his hand cupping the back of my head as I wept. "Are you okay? Did I do something wrong?"

"My goodness, no," I cried. "You did everything right. You are the most amazing man I have ever met." Tears poured from my eyes. The front of his shirt was soaked.

"You can't begin to understand my happiness right now. No one has ever done anything like this for me. Ever. Oh my goodness, I have to sit down."

Joseph held me tight and walked me to the edge of bed. I sank into the mattress, closing my eyes. He knelt in front of me and held my hands in his own.

"The hard part's over, Jamie. We just have to get people to come here and we're set."

My gaze flew to his. How could I run two coffee shops? How could I choose between the business I started on my own and the one that Joseph generously built with his own sweat, blood, and money? I couldn't fathom closing down the one in Cincinnati. "How are we going to do this? Please don't think I'm being selfish, but I don't want to close the coffee shop I already own."

"You won't have to. I've already taken care of it. You know that friend I was setting Melissa up with? Well, that was my way of getting her cell number, so I could run it by her. And she's agreed to manage the Cinci shop, so you can live here."

"What about you?" I clutched his hands and panicked at the thought of living two hours away from where Joseph lived and worked. "I can't live here without you."

"We'll make it work. Don't worry, I'll be here every weekend."

Weekends weren't enough. I needed to be with him every day. Then it occurred to me. Of course, he would be close by. I reached into my back pocket and pulled out the envelope. His name decorated the front in bold calligraphy.

"What's this?" he asked.

"It's my Valentine's gift to you. Think of it as a way to keep you from commuting from Cinci to Lexington."

He narrowed his eyes as he pulled out the check. I watched his face furrow for a second and then draw backward. His brows lifted in surprise and disbelief. "Am I looking at this right?"

I smiled. "Seems you're not the only with a plan, Joseph. Your uncle's not buying the farm tomorrow. I am. You just have to be there to sign your name on the deed."

"Jamie, I can't afford two mortgages on my salary. I just took out a loan to buy your grandma's house. The bank won't give me any more money."

"You won't need anymore. I'm buying it."

"Does Miranda know about this?"

I knew it was hard for him to think she'd agree to sell to someone outside the family. "Of course, she did. How else could I do this? My name won't be on the deed, because I want it to be yours, free and clear. I'm just the bank."

"Jamie, this is too much. You can't—"

"I can and I already have. Trust me, it's not going to break me. I'm making money hand over fist with the coffee shop in Cinci. And this bed and breakfast will surely pull in more revenue. The first year is always the hardest," I admitted. "But, I bet I could draw people in by hiring...oh, I don't know...a hot superintendent slash grounds keeper slash bellman who lives right down the road from here."

He laughed at my idea, but I think I had him sold— especially the part about living right down the road. He ran his hand through his hair as he stared at the numbers on the check.

"Joseph?" He looked at me and I could see the emotion swirling in his Montana blue-sky eyes. I pulled him closer to me, my knees on either side of his ribs. He pulled me closer to him, as I wound my hands around his neck, playing with the hair at his nape. "Say you'll sign it."

He started to shake his head, seemingly undecided, but I cupped his face and redirected his attention. "Look at me, Joseph. I want this for you. I want to give you back the land you should've never parted with. If I didn't need your signature on the deed, I would've already bought it for you and we wouldn't be having this discussion. But given real estate law, I can't purchase it without your John Hancock."

"Are you asking me to quit my job in Cinci and move here with you?"

"Yes," I said matter-of-factly. "Quit your job, move here, and work for me."

"Is it really that simple?" he asked.

"It's only difficult if we let it be." And I truly believed that. Finding the man of my dreams had been the most daunting task of my life. But building a life with that man, knowing he loved me enough to forsake his own dreams, would be a piece of cake. As far as I could see, there was nothing ahead of us but blue skies.

"Truth or dare, Jamie?" His question came out of nowhere.

"What?"

"Answer me. Truth or dare. And then I'll agree to sign."

I looked at him sideways, unable to predict where he was going with this. We'd already played 'truth' by coming clean on the selfless gifts we'd schemed behind each other's backs. Maybe he wanted something a bit more intimate than just confessing truths. Looking at the handsome man kneeling before me, I was ready for something that required a bit more action. "Okay, let's go dare this time."

His mouth kicked up in a devious smile as he yanked his shirt from his body and tossed it aside. My mouth went dry gazing at his beautiful muscled chest and shoulders.

"I dare you..." He placed his hands on my upper arms and urged me backward until I was totally reclined on the bed. He climbed over my body until we were eye to eye. "I dare you, Jamett Penelope Sutherland..."

My eyes widened as I heard my hideous birth name. I was going to kick Melissa's ass for that slip. I just knew it was her who told Joseph my real name.

His hot mouth dove to mine. Every thought scattered as he smothered them all with his kiss. I thought of nothing but his warm, velvety tongue sliding along mine and the solid, muscled body pressing me into the pillow top mattress.

His hand gripped my shirt and pulled it over my head. Breathlessly, he whispered, "I dare you to..." His eyes opened in surprise as he took notice of the lacy red bra I wore. He groaned and dove back to kissing me. His mouth trailed to my neck, and I was helpless to fend him off, even if I had wanted to. The feel of his warm lips, wet tongue, and rough prickly beard had me begging for more.

With the merest of brain function left, I was dying to know what he wanted of me. "You dare me to what, Joseph?"

I moved beneath him, feeling his hot skin against mine. He pulled away and his eyes darkened. A great, tumultuous storm raged in them. "Marry me, Sutherland."

Silence slammed into the room. Only the ticking of Grandma's grandfather clock in the hallway disturbed the hush of this moment for I swear my heart stopped. Was I dreaming? Was this man—the man who had me at "Welcome to the building, Jamie;" the man who gave his whole heart to me; the man who'd already made my wildest dreams come true—asking me to marry him?

"Did you hear me?"

"Yes."

"Yes, as in yes, you heard me? Or yes, you'll marry me?"

I stared into his beautiful eyes and felt my heart pitter patter against my ribs. I smiled as he lay upon me, his breath held, his body tense. I'd never seen Joseph Alexander Scarbrough so nervous.

"Yes, I'll marry you," I whispered, caressing his gorgeous face.

I felt his body relax and he sighed, his lips pressing against mine. His arms snaked around me and pulled me against his chest. I felt his mouth at my ear, his heated breath bathing my skin.

"I love you, Joseph," I whispered, my body quivering beneath his touch.

A mischievous chuckle shook his body. "I dare you to prove it."

His hand blazed a path down my side and caught the waistband of my jeans. He tugged on the zipper and my breath caught. I heard his boots hit the floor in the same moment his knuckles grazed my tummy. I shuddered at his intimate touch. I knew it was going to be one seriously long, wholly satisfying, blazing hot night with a man who knew exactly what he was doing.

There was only one thing Joseph needed to learn. And that was never to call me by my real name.

No worries though. I had two icing-heaped cupcakes still sitting in a box to help me get that point across.

THE END

If you enjoyed this book by Renee Vincent, please consider leaving an honest review at your favorite vendor. Reviews not only give credibility to an author's work, they also help other readers find quality books worth reading.

About Renee Vincent

RENEE VINCENT is a *USA Today* bestselling author of romance and women's fiction. Her books have earned numerous accolades, including a #1 Bestseller for Viking Romance.

She lives on a secluded hundred-acre horse farm in the rolling hills of Kentucky with her husband, two beautiful daughters, a couple of nocturnal dogs, and a pair of cats who think they're the masters of the house. Truth be told…they are.

www.ReneeVincent.com

Books By Series

Vikings of Honor Series
Sunset Fire, Book 1
Emerald Glory, Book 2
Souls Reborn, Book 3
Tempered Steel, Book 4

Mavericks of Meeteetse Series
Longing for Langston, Brody & Liv, Book 1
Made for McKinley, Jonas & Ava, Book 2
Falling For Forester, Cole & Crys, Book 3
Wild for Wallace, Sawyer & Charlotte, Book 4

Jamett & Joseph Series
The Start of Something Good, Book 1
The Road to Something Better, Book 2
The Gift of Something Grand, Book 3

Stand Alone Novel
Silent Partner

Mailing List

Sign up for Renee Vincent's author newsletter and reap the benefits of being one of her loyal subscribers! One lucky winner is drawn each month. What's more, you get a FREE BOOK just for joining.

Go to ReneeVincent.com, then click on "Newsletter" to sign up and start reading!

ReneeVincent.com

www.ingramcontent.com/pod-product-compliance
Lightning Source LLC
Chambersburg PA
CBHW021046130626
46552CB00005B/2030